U the Pig Nut Tree

Edward L. Schultz

MW01535438

J.W.
Thanks for
your encouragement.
Edd Shultz
Feb 2014

© 2013 by Edward L. Schultz.
All rights reserved. No part of this book may be reproduced, stored in a retrieval system or transmitted in any form or by any means without the prior written permission of the publisher, except by a reviewer who may quote brief passages in a review to be printed in a newspaper, magazine or journal.

First Edition

ISBN: 9781482773866
PUBLISHED BY EDWARD L. SCHULTZ
Willoughby, OH

Printed in the Unites States

Additional copies available from Amazon.com
Also available in Kindle edition

Dedicated to my father. I wish I had known him better.

Prologue

I felt a deep sense of panic.

My sister was asleep. My mother was out with her Bridge Club, but my father was watching television. I crept down the stairs, tears dropping from my cheeks down to my pajama tops. I walked into the den where Pa was watching something, but what program it was didn't register with me.

"What's the matter, Butch?" he asked. I always liked it when he called me 'Butch.'

In a small voice, I answered, "Abraham Lincoln's dead."

"Yeah?"

"And I'm gonna die some day, too," I managed to get out before the tears streamed down my face.

In my third-grade class, we had just been learning about Abraham Lincoln. We learned something new about him every day for a week. I liked Lincoln a lot. At the end of the week, we were told that he was killed by John Wilkes Booth. At that moment, it didn't seem that bad, but that night when I went to bed it was all I could think of. Abraham Lincoln was dead. Abraham Lincoln was dead. Then it occurred to me that if Abraham Lincoln was dead, then some day *I* would be dead, too.

Without saying a word, my father reached down, scooped me up into his arms and sat me on his lap. He held me in his arms. He positioned me so that we could both watch the TV and he continued to hold me. I felt the warmth of his body. I could smell the tobacco, and it was somehow comforting.

Chapter One

It was the summer of 1960 and I was eleven years old. This was the last day of school. We only had a half day. The pig nut tree was straight and tall. It sat in the middle of a small clearing, surrounded by tall grass. If you looked to one side you could see a few houses maybe a half mile away, but, if you looked the other way...it was like being on top of the world. You could see for miles off into the distance. There was a very steep hill on that side. At the bottom of the hill were houses, but you couldn't see them when you sat under the pig nut tree. It was always quiet up there.

"Johnny Jet's faster than the Flash," said Douglas, leaning up against the tree and staring off into space.

"But, how could he be faster than the Flash?" I asked. "The Flash is the fastest man alive."

"Well," replied my friend, "I made him up, so he can be as fast as I want him to be. I hosey he's faster than the Flash."

"I don't know. I have an idea. How about if he drives a real fast car, too? Like a jet car. That way he's different than the Flash."

My mind immediately began to reel with ideas about what the car would look like. And it had to be blue. Johnny Jet had to wear a blue costume. The Flash wore a red one.

Douglas Collier sat down next to me and scooped up a pig nut in his hand. He found a flat rock, carefully placed the nut on it, then smashed the shell with a second rock. He pried the meat out of the nut and popped it into his mouth. He wiped off his hands and then brushed the front of his hair. Like all of us, Doug had a crew cut, although we called it a whiffle. He got a little frustrated because it wasn't staying up.

"Gimme your whiffle stick," he demanded. So, I dug in my pocket and produced a short stick of waxy material. Doug took it from me and used it to push up the front of his hair. The hair stood up straight. Now he was cool.

It was only the beginning of summer and we were already bored. Doug turned in my direction.

"Let's go home. I'm bored. Besides, it's almost time for supper probably."

I agreed. I had no idea what time it was, because I didn't have a watch, but we could tell by the sun and the traffic that we could see down below on Quincy Avenue that people were going home after work.

So, we walked back down Pleasantview Avenue. It was only about a half mile. It was a walk that we had taken many, many times before. The pig nut tree was one of our favorite places to go because it was so quiet.

Mine was the second house from the bottom of the street. Doug's was on the main street, Quincy Ave, touching my back yard. We walked beside my house, between our two Macintosh apple trees and into the back yard. Then we sat down for a minute on the old wooden picnic table. We were only there for a few seconds when my father pulled into the driveway with his green and white station wagon.

Pa got out of the car, tugging on Laddie's leash. The friskie young beagle jumped down onto the ground. As soon as I saw him, I rolled my eyes up into my head. I hated that dog. Laddie didn't really do anything wrong, but I hated him because my father loved him. My father took him to work every day. He could do that because he had his own business, a sign shop. He was a very talented craftsman. He had been painting signs for a long time. I called him Pa because I was angry with him. Up until about a year before, I had called him either Dad or Daddy, but then I began to call him Pa as my quiet way of protesting.

I gave a wave of acknowledgment, but my heart sank almost immediately. I saw the expression on his face at the same time that I spotted the lawn mower. I knew what I had forgotten, and I knew how he was going to react.

"Eddy, get over here!" he called with his deep, somewhat gruff voice.

"Guess I'd better go," said Doug. "See you tomorrow." He jumped off the picnic table and headed to the fence that divided our yards, pushed aside a loose board and entered his own yard.

Reluctantly I stepped to the ground and walked toward the house.

"What the hell have you been doing all day? I thought I told you to mow the lawn before I got home tonight."

"I had some trouble getting it started," was my excuse. "Then Doug came over and I just lost track of time."

Laddie strained on the leash, trying to greet me, but my father held him back.

"I bet you did," was Pa's impatient response. I always lost track of time. This wasn't the first time he heard me say that, nor would it be

6

the last. "Well, get to work now and do as much as you can before your mother gets home. And don't do a half-assed job."

I hated it when he said that. "Half-assed job," I mumbled under my breath as father and canine "son" went through the back door and into the kitchen.

I guess I hated a lot of things in those days, because I hated cutting the grass, too. I hated the lawn mower. It never started for me. Anyway, I went to the back shed and took out the metal can of gasoline, opened the mower's fuel tank and topped it off. I opened the choke, pushed on the primer a few times, then pulled the cord that was supposed to start the motor. Cough, cough, sput! Shit! Try again. Cough, cough, sput! Cough, cough, sput! I hated that lawn mower.

The back door opened and my father hastily came down the steps.

"Let me do it."

With an expert tug, he pulled the cord and the mower started up. No problem.

"Now get to work!" he shouted over the drone of the motor and went back into the house, shaking his head from side to side and muttering something that I couldn't hear.

Mowing the lawn was the most boring, monotonous thing that anyone could do. Back and forth. Back and forth. *Be sure you do a good job around the trees. Don't accidentally cut your mother's flowers. Be careful of the curb along the driveway. Watch out for rocks and branches. Don't always cut in the same direction. Make sure you overlap.*

Once in a while, to make the job a little more palatable I would imagine that someone was asking my advice about grass cutting, and that I was an expert. I'd try to come up with different techniques for mowing more efficiently or more quickly. Such fantasies seemed to help a little...but not much.

Finally...saved. My mother arrived home. She waved me over as she got out of the car. I gladly left the stinky machine running.

"You can stop mowing now," she said. "Put the mower in the back yard and get ready for supper."

She didn't give me any grief. Although my mother frequently told me that I was lazy, she didn't usually yell at me or get very angry. She just sighed with frustration. Mom was a secretary, which is probably why she knew how to work with people better than Pa did.

I had no hesitation about stopping the mower and putting it

7

away. I figured that my father would rather have me work until dark without any supper, but when my mother gave an order, everyone obeyed. She was short, not quite five feet tall, but she was a powerhouse. So, I walked the mower to the back, went in through the cellar door and up the steps to the kitchen. As soon as I opened the door I was greeted with a question and a command.

"Did you lock the cellar door?" my father inquired.

"Go wash your hands," stated my mother.

"Yes, I locked the cellar door," I sighed. "Okay, I'll wash my hands."

"Supper will be ready in a few minutes," Mom announced. "In the meantime, Eddy, why don't you go upstairs and clean your room like I told you to do today? I don't know why you never do it when I tell you to. And do a good job, so I don't have to do it over."

I closed my eyes and just sighed. My mother was a perfectionist, and she liked to have a spic and span house. When she woke up in the morning, she would clean the house. Then, when she got home from work, she'd clean it again...because the dust had settled! *GOOD HOUSEKEEPING Magazine* could call any time, without any notice, and drop in to do a photo shoot and the house would be immaculate. Well, those statements are both exaggerations, but I think you get the point. I always admired my mother's thoroughness and cleanliness, but it was a pain in the neck to try to keep up with it or to try to meet her expectations.

I trudged upstairs to my bedroom. I had twin beds, although one of them was rarely used, since my sister had moved into her own room, across from mine. We probably kept the bed there because there was nowhere else to put it. From time to time, I would sleep in the second bed, but usually only if I didn't feel like making my own bed.

My room wasn't big, but I liked it. The two beds, a desk and chair, a stuffed armchair, a TV (black & white, of course and only because we had recently bought a bigger, newer one), three closets, a small bookcase, and a big, built-in chest of drawers. The closets weren't very roomy and they had curtains instead of doors.

As I looked around, trying to decide where to start cleaning, I spotted my Mattel Fanner 50 cap gun and holster, draped over my stuffed chair. This had been one of my favorite toys for several years. It was one of the most authentic cap guns made, being about the same size as a real six-shooter, although it was chrome rather than black like the ones used by most TV cowboys. The belt and holster were made of "genuine leather" and had loops into which you could put toy bullets. The leather was tan, instead of the black or dark brown also used by most TV cowboys. I hadn't played with this in several months.

I took the holster off the chair and strapped it on, being sure to tie the leather thong around my right thigh. The cowboy hat was next. This was a genuine 10 gallon Stetson that had belonged to my father. It was still just a tiny bit large, but it served its purpose. In fact, it served many purposes. I could use it as a straight cowboy hat, or pin up the brim in the front to be a Pony Express rider or Texas John Slaughter, or pin it up on the side to be a Musketeer or The Gray Ghost (Major John Singleton Mosby), or pin it up on three sides to be Johnny Tremain or Paul Revere. My only disappointment in the hat was its color - tan. I wished that it could have been black. For some reason, I felt that tan was a kid's color and black was a grown-up color.

Slowly, my hand went up and down the side of the holster, caressing it. My feet spread slightly apart so that my balance was good.

Suddenly, my hand flashed up, grabbed hold of the pistol and drew it from the holster. I just held it out and stared at my imaginary foe.

"This is a Colt .45," I said softly and deliberately. "It'll put a hole in you the size of a grapefruit. I don't want to pull the trigger, but if you don't leave town right now, I will...who am I?...what's my name? My name is Paladin!"

My revery was abruptly interrupted by my sister's voice.

"What are you doing in there, you jerk? Mommy told you to clean your room."

After clicking my tongue impatiently, I answered, "Just shut up and go away, Donna!"

"I will *not* shut up! Supper's ready!"

I guess I hadn't been talking to myself as softly as I thought.

My sister Donna was two years older. She was a typical older sister...bossy! As a teenager, she thought she was hot stuff. When she was younger, she was often mistaken for Annette Funicello, the *Mouseketeer*. Donna did look a little bit like Annette. I, on the other hand, did not look like anyone on *The Mickey Mouse Club* TV show. If I resembled anyone on TV it was Alfalfa from *The Little Rascals*! Skinny, a cowlick in my hair and freckles on my cheeks.

I often took delight in teasing my sister. I was a big fan of horror movies and Donna hated them. So, occasionally, I would hide in her bedroom closet then jump out and scare her. I even had this one

9

running gag stunt that always succeeded in scaring the wits out of her. We had seen a movie called *The Nanny* with Bette Davis as an evil babysitter who tried to smother the children with a pillow. So, when I wanted to get the best of Donna, I would hold up a pillow (especially when she was already in bed) and say menacingly, "Donna, would you like another pillow?" She would scream and I would chuckle.

Suppertime for our family was a very quiet time. My father had been raised in an environment where no one spoke at the dinner table. While he wasn't quite as rigid as his upbringing, most of our meals were eaten with very little conversation. What did make mealtime a pleasure was my mother's cooking! She was a great cook. Steak (medium rare), roast beef, roast pork, fried chicken (very seldom, because Pa didn't really care for chicken), accompanied by mashed potatoes, gravy, various vegetables, and always some kind of dessert, usually baked from scratch. Mom was a great baker, too! Chocolate devil's food cake with chocolate frosting, brownies, toll house cookies, cupcakes. One of my favorite meals was spaghetti and meatballs. My mother's parents had immigrated from Sicily, so any time we had Italian food of any kind, it was authentic and delicious. We had it all and it was all great...except for the occasional liver. Blah! My sister and I usually drank milk, often flavored with Hershey's Chocolate Syrup. Mom and Dad had coffee. Hers included milk and sugar. His was always accompanied by evaporated milk and *no* sugar! Real men don't sweeten their coffee!

After eating, my sister and I took turns washing and drying the dishes. This was not one of my favorite chores, but, then, I don't think I did actually have a favorite.

Then, we settled into our usual Friday night routine. My mother would get out the ironing board and start ironing the laundry. My father, sister and I would sit down in the den and watch television. Pa and Donna would sit on opposite ends of the couch, he with his feet stretched out onto the hassock. I would lie down on the floor, with my head leaning against the hassock.

At 7:30 we watched *Rawhide*, starring Eric Fleming and Clint Eastwood. This was the ongoing story of a cattle drive. With the thrilling theme song sung by Frankie Laine, we got in the mood for lots of western excitement. This was a time of westerns and detective stories, the most popular TV genres of the early sixties. My father and I both especially liked westerns. I knew that deep in his heart, Pa really wanted to be a cowboy. As a young man he had ridden horses and worked in a stable. He liked shooting guns of all kinds. On one occasion when he and my mother went to a costume party, they both dressed up in western gear, and we remarked that he looked like the actor Randolph Scott, with his ten gallon, tan Stetson hat and a neckerchief tied around his throat.

At 8:30 *Hotel DeParee* was the next western, although it wasn't our top choice. The star, Earl Holliman, had a strange way about him. Neither of us cared for his character, but we watched the show nevertheless.

One of my all-time favorite shows came on at 9:00, *77 Sunset Strip*, with Efrem Zimbalist, Jr., Roger Smith and Edd Byrnes. The detective agency of Bailey and Spencer intrigued us each week. However, in this case, my fascination was not with the detective work, but rather with the very popular character played by Edd Byrnes. Gerald Lloyd Kookson, III, also known as "Kookie" was the object of my admiration. Kookie was a sort of beatnik or hipster who served as parking lot attendant and was himself an aspiring private eye. His casual style and hip slang caught everyone's attention. He was "cool, man, cool." In fact, he was the "ginchiest!" He was always whipping out his comb to style his hair ("Kookie, Kookie, lend me your comb"), wore his collar up and was often "piling up the Zs." Byrnes was such an inspiration to me that I began spelling my own first name "Edd" instead of "Ed." I was past the stage where "Eddy" was acceptable. After all, for many years my father was known among relatives as Big Eddy and I was Little Eddy. Enough of that!

Because it wasn't a school night, I was allowed to stay up late. The 10:00 show was a toss-up between *The Twilight Zone* or *The Detectives*. Sometimes Rod Serling's sci-fi series would scare the beegeebers out of me, but most of the time it was just a fascinating trip into the realms of imagination. Pa preferred *The Detectives*, and, of course, he won out whenever he wanted to.

We ended the night at 10:30 with *The Law and Mr. Jones*, starring James Whitmore as an attorney. I always liked Whitmore's eyebrows. They were bushy, much like my father's. They gave his face a lot of character.

Television was very important to me. If life seemed a little humdrum or boring, at least I could imaginatively live out my fantasies with the characters I saw on the small screen. In many ways, TV was also educational. The stories about American history or science fiction inspired me to explore the reality behind the fantasy.

11

Chapter Two

Saturday mornings were usually bowling time. Doug and I would walk down to Weymouth Landing, maybe a four mile trek, to go candlepin bowling. The bowling alley was literally tucked away in an alley between several small department stores. We were always welcomed by Buddy, the manager. He was very short, somewhat stout, had bright red, balding hair, glasses and "buggy" eyes. He was kind of creepy-looking, but he was always cordial.

Our allowances generally only allowed us to bowl two games, but that was enough to keep us busy for about an hour.

"You know what I don't understand," I said after our second game. "I don't understand why we have to turn in the score sheet every time we play. I don't know why we can't just take it home with us...like for a souvenir."

Doug had an idea. Down toward the bottom of the sheet there was plenty of room for him to copy the scores, making a copy for each of us to take home. He tore the bottom of the sheet off and stuffed it into his shirt.

"That's easy!" he said confidently. Although I felt a little bit uneasy about this, neither of us figured that we had done anything wrong.

When we were finished, we hastily turned in our shoes, placed the score sheet on the counter and put our money on top. Buddy was busy, so he just waved us off. We left the alley as was our custom. We'd probably stop at the library on the way home.

"Hey! Youse kids! Come back here!" shouted Buddy. When we turned, we saw that his face was flushed and his eyes were buggier than usual. He was holding our score sheet in one hand. We were in trouble.

"You're trying to cheat me. Yez played extra games and didn't pay for 'em."

"No, we didn't," I countered. "We just...."

"Gimme the rest of the score sheet!" he demanded.

I saw Doug's face. He was shaken. His eyes began to fill with tears as he reached into his shirt to retrieve the document. That was strange, because Doug usually seemed to be fearless. This was one of the reasons that I admired him so much.

"Honest, Buddy," he sobbed. "We weren't cheating, we just wanted to take home a copy of our scores. We just copied them. Look at it and you can see for yourself."

Buddy took the paper in his chubby hands, opened it quickly and scanned the page. He calmed down.

"Maybe so, but don't youse two ever try to cheat me...or I'll call the cops on yez."

Then, he turned and plodded back to the bowling alley. That was the last time we went bowling.

Before returning home, Doug had an idea.

"Hey, let's go check out the old movie theater!"

Just a few blocks away was an abandoned movie theater. It had been closed for several years. It was dark and spooky. Just the thing that two young boys would find attractive. I quickly changed my demeanor to something very serious.

"Say, Frank, do you think there might be some pirate treasure hidden there?" I asked.

"There might be, Joe. It's worth exploring...let's go!"

We were now Frank and Joe Hardy - The Hardy Boys, off on an adventure. Although the *Mickey Mouse Club* had been off the air for a year, *The Hardy Boys* had been one of our favorite serials. Doug was taller than I, and sort of looked like Tim Considine. I wasn't as chubby as Tommy Kirk, but he was one of my favorite Disney actors.

We cased the joint from outside, and noticed that one of the front doors seemed to be ajar. Several minutes went by before the coast was clear - no adults looking. So, we tried the door. Open! We jumped inside the lobby as quickly as we could and ducked down low to escape detection from anyone who might be walking by.

"This is really cool!" I whispered. My body was shaking in a combination of fear and excitement. I could see that my companion was feeling the same way.

"Wish we had a flashlight," he said.

The theater was dark, but enough light came in from the front doors to allow us to make our way around the lobby, and when we opened one of the doors into the theater, the light poured into the darkness. A dank, musty odor stung inside our noses. The floor was littered with old candy wrappers and popcorn boxes. Many of the seats were torn up. I crouched down low. Doug stood up and walked confidently down the aisle.

"Hello!" he called.

"Shut up, Frank!" I whispered as loud as I could. "Someone might hear us and we'll get in trouble."

"Don't worry, Joe," he replied. "There's no one here."

Suddenly, there was a splashing sound from down near the screen. We both jumped and "Frank" ran back up the aisle toward me. We both cowered behind some seats. We waited a long time, but there was no other sound.

"It was probably just some water from a leak in the old roof," my partner assured me.

We decided to go upstairs and check out the balcony. We crept slowly along the wall, because there wasn't very much light coming into the stairway. The walls felt cruddy and dirty. Finally, we made it to the doorway and inside. We didn't dare walk very far because it was so dark and we were afraid we'd fall.

"Hey, let's make out," whispered Doug. "Smoochie. Smoochie."

"Are you crazy?" I replied. Then he started chuckling.

"I was only kidding. But, just think about it. This is where kids always go to make out."

He was right. At least that was what I had been told. The only reason you sit in the balcony is to make out with a girl, not to watch the movie. Just the thought of making out was creepy.

"Maybe we better get going soon," was all I could say.

"Not before getting some souvenirs," Doug said. "Come on!"

Carefully we made our way back down the stairs, and keeping low to the ground, we snuck into the ticket booth. There were rolls of tickets. Doug stuffed some into his pockets, as did I. I spotted some film canisters, pried one open and found several feet of 16 mm film.

"Hey, look at this!"

I unrolled a section and held it up to the light. It was a movie of someone doing gymnastics. We both squinted and looked through it. Once we were done, I rolled it back up and stashed it in my front pocket.

"Okay, Joe," said my fellow boy detective, "Let's get outta here now before we get caught!"

"Good idea, Frank," I said.

Just as I said that, we could hear a door creaking open. We peered back into the theater and could see some light. Someone was opening one of the exit doors. We could just make out a guy wearing a baseball cap. I signaled to Doug to be quiet. We both froze for what seemed to be an hour. The guy didn't seem to be moving either. He just looked from side to side. Then the door closed. We still didn't move because we weren't sure if the guy was inside the theater or out. My heart was thumping so fast and hard that I thought I was going to pass out. And, I had to pee!

Finally, we decided that the coast was clear. But, my bladder was aching. I started looking around.

"What are you looking for?" Doug asked.

"I'm looking for the men's room. I have to take a leak."

"Get real. I have to take a piss, too, but there's no one around. We don't need a men's room."

He stood up and walked into the darkened theater. I heard a *zip* as my friend opened his fly and began to relieve himself. I joined him. The sprinkling echoed throughout the old building, as did our quiet laughter.

Getting out was more difficult than getting in. From our vantage point in the lobby, we weren't really able to see if anyone was walking down the sidewalk, or driving by. We took turns sticking our heads up. Finally, Doug yelled "Now!" and we bolted for the door. Once outside, we ran around the corner into an alley and immediately slowed our pace. We sighed with relief. Doug bent over, with his hands on his thighs.

"That was a close call!"

I was still trembling.

"Sure was!"

It was still early enough so that we could stop at the library on our way home. On the corner of a small strip of stores sat the small local branch library. "East Braintree Library" read the sign over the door. As we walked inside we were greeted by the two older ladies who served as librarians. The library had the delicious odor of old books. This smelled much better than the theater. Every time I entered the building, it was like walking into another world, another dimension. The walls were covered with possible new worlds and new adventures. I wished that I could just sit there and read every single book.

"Hello, Edward. Hello, Douglas," said Miss Giles in her soft, southern accent. She was very tall, probably in her seventies, not very good-looking, but very nice. She looked like a typical spinster-librarian - hair pulled back in a bun, glasses on a chain around her neck. Well, we called her an "old lady librarian" but that wasn't very nice.

"Hello, Miss Giles," I returned.

The other librarian, whose name I could never remember, waved me over.

"Edward, when Miss Giles and I were at the main library, we found a book that you might like to read."

I was always in the library. And my choice of books was not typical. Whenever I would see something on television or in the movies that interested me, I wanted to read everything I could about it. So, I would go to the library and ask. If they didn't have a book on the subject at our branch, these two thoughtful women would check the main library, where they each worked one or two days a week.

The librarian handed me an old blue, cloth-covered book. I looked at the spine to see the title. **Houdini: The Man Who Walked Through Walls**.

"We know that you're interested in magic, so we thought you might like to read a biography of one of the most famous magicians of all time," she said with a smile.

Wow! I thought. I had heard of Houdini before and had read a little bit about him in comic books and in *Boy's Life* magazine. But, here was a whole book about his life. A feeling of tremendous excitement rose in my chest. I could hardly speak.

"Thank you so much! This is great! Thank you!"

My excitement was very obvious.

"You're quite welcome, Edward," the librarian replied with a satisfied smile.

I immediately went over to the table, sat down and began to thumb through the book, looking at the chapter titles and illustrations. In the meantime, Doug was browsing through the science fiction section. Although he enjoyed watching me do magic tricks sometimes, my friend didn't usually share my interest in magic. But, he *loved* science fiction.

Doug came over to the table and plopped a book on top of the one I was reading.

"If you want to read a really great book, read this one...**Lucky Starr and the Oceans of Venus** by Isaac Asimov," he pronounced. "It's one of the best science fiction books ever written."

I must admit that I liked science fiction, too. At that point, my favorite book in that genre was **The Red Planet** by Robert Heinlein. It was the story of a kid on Mars named Jim Marlowe. The coolest thing about the story was a strange creature named Willis, which was a fuzzy, round being about the size of a basketball. It had a photographic memory and could "play back" "recordings" of what anyone had said...in their own voice. Needless to say, Willis got Jim into a lot of trouble. I liked the book so much that I even wrote a letter to a movie studio suggesting that they consider making a film of the book...*and by the way, I wouldn't mind playing the role of Jim, even though I don't have any acting experience*. Surprisingly enough, I did later receive a letter from someone at the studio letting me know that they were busy with other projects. No comment on my willingness to play the starring role, though.

I thanked Doug for his suggestion and put this book under my Houdini biography. I would certainly check them both out. And so, I did. They both soon became favorites. The Houdini book was one that I especially treasured and renewed many times. In the center were several pages of photographs of Houdini at various stages of his career. I wanted to have pictures of my hero in my room. So, I did something that would cause me to feel guilty for many years to come. Using a razor blade, I very carefully cut two pictures out of the book. One picture of Houdini and his wife Bess was pasted into my scrap book. The other, a picture of Houdini in chains, I framed and put up on my wall, hoping that my parents would never notice it and ask where it came from. When I later returned the book to the library, I felt like a criminal because I had defaced library property. But, I never said a word to anyone about what I had done and no one seemed the wiser.

Chapter Three

Saturday night was also a big night for television...a mixed night of westerns and drama. At 7:30 we had to choose between three shows that we all liked. The court room drama of *Perry Mason* inspired me, briefly, to want to become a lawyer. I especially liked the courtroom scenes where the murderer would finally be revealed. Strangely enough, it was seldom the person on trial. Sometimes we chose to change the channel and watch *The Roaring Twenties*. Of course, I had a tremendous crush on Pinky Pinkham, the flapper/singer played by Dorothy Provine. I even saved her picture from the cover of *TV Guide*! Usually, however, we watched *Bonanza*, the story of a family of men who lived and worked on the big Ponderosa Ranch...a western, of course. On the few Saturday nights that Pa wasn't home, I preferred to watch *The Roaring Twenties*.

Then at 8:30 we had another choice between favorites. Either we could watch the detective show *Checkmate* for a full hour or two half hour westerns, *The Tall Man* with Barry Sullivan and Clu Gulager as Pat Garret and Billy the Kid, and *The Deputy* starring Henry Fonda. When Pa was home the westerns always won out. However, I really liked *Checkmate*, especially the character Dr. Carl Hyatt, played by Sebastian Cabot. He was a criminologist, not just an ordinary detective. Perhaps my interest in Sherlock Holmes was what caused my fascination with this character. Both men had an uncanny way of deducing the solution to the crime. I wished that I had those kinds of skills.

At 9:30 was my all-time favorite western...*Have Gun, Will Travel* starring Richard Boone as Paladin. Paladin was a gunfighter, a gun for hire, in fact. He had two "identities." He lived in San Francisco at a very exclusive hotel, the Carlton. While there he wore fancy clothes, ruffled shirts and a bell-crown top hat. You might call him a dandy. He smoked cigars and was often accompanied by beautiful women. Paladin would go to the opera or ballet, eat fine food, and even engage in a game of poker now and then. My father never seemed to approve much of this aspect of Paladin's life. I would occasionally hear a soft "Hmph!" from Pa when Paladin would appear in his gentleman's attire.

Frequently, Paladin would be browsing through his newspaper and find an advertisement looking for a hired gun, or an article about someone in danger or trouble. He would cut out the ad and give it, along with his business card (which read: *Have Gun Will Travel, Wire Paladin, San Francisco*, and sported a white chess knight logo) to Hey Boy, the Chinese hotel attendant, with instructions to send this to the person in question. The scene would shift and Paladin would now be dressed all in black, six shooter on his hip, and black cowboy hat on his head. This was what Pa wanted to see.

I often thought that Pa bore a slight resemblance to Richard Boone, although my father was better-looking. I think that Pa liked Paladin because he was rugged and a no-nonsense kind of person. He always got the job done, although he seemed to dislike violence. Strange for a man who made his living with a gun.

One of the aspects of Paladin's personality that attracted me was his quotations from literature, especially Shakespeare. That was really cool. It showed that he was a man of letters as well as a man of action. This inspired me to ask my sixth grade teacher, Mr. Gregory, about Shakespeare. He was duly impressed by my interest. When I asked him what play I should read first, he suggested *The Merchant of Venice*, which I promptly asked for at the library. Soon I read other plays and was able to occasionally quote the Bard, just like Paladin.

Paladin was followed by Pa's favorite, *Gunsmoke,* starring James Arness as Marshall Matt Dillon. Marshall Dillon was another no-nonsense cowboy who seemed to be hesitant to use gun-play to solve a problem, but he often did have to resort to shooting the bad guy. Not a word was spoken during either of these shows, except for the pauses allowed by commercials.

Of course, my father and I both had one cowboy hero who was above all the rest - Roy Rogers, King of the Cowboys. From a very young age, I had watched Roy, Dale, Trigger, Bullet, Pat Brady and the Double R Bar Ranch, and had sung their theme song with them. *"Happy trails to you, until we meet again...."* I even remember Pa singing the song with me. I thought my father looked a little like Roy Rogers.

During the school year, we used to go to church on Sunday mornings, at least until my sister was confirmed. Donna decided that once that had happened, she was too old to go to Sunday School. But, I had to go. So, for some strange reason, I ended up being the only one who went to church. Everyone else stayed home (except for Palm Sunday and Easter) and I got a ride to church from Mrs. Parry, an elderly woman who lived up the street. She was a Sunday School teacher, so she had to be there every Sunday.

After church we would all go to my Grandparent's house for Sunday dinner. I really enjoyed that. Grandma and Grandpa (on my mother's side) had come to America from Sicily when they were children, but they still didn't speak very much English. Grandpa actually only spoke Italian.

This was a real gathering of the clan. My mother had two brothers and two sisters, so there were plenty of aunts and uncles...and cousins. A few of my cousins were older and a few were younger, but there were four of us who had been born in the same year. I was the oldest, being born in July. Then there were Glenny and Joel, and Nancy was the only girl. The three of us boys hung out together whenever the family gathered.

There was always a lot of noise. Italians love to talk and laugh and eat. At any one time there would be at least a dozen or more people sitting around the crowded dining room table. There would be all sorts of food - especially spaghetti. There was *always* spaghetti. If we had roast beef, there was spaghetti. If we had ham, there was spaghetti. "Mangiare! Mangiare!" Grandma would always say. "Eat! Eat!"

One special treat that we would all fight over was Grandma's meatless meatballs. They were made of breadcrumbs, cheese and eggs. They were so delicious that *everyone* wanted them. Who would get the last one?

If it was raining, then late Sunday afternoon usually consisted of my being firmly planted in front of the TV watching old war movies or swashbuckling adventure movies. Humphrey Bogart, James Cagney, Patrick O'Brien, Errol Flynn, knights, pirates, Musketeers, Count of Monte Cristo, Robin Hood...they all became my heroes. But, if the weather was sunny, my mother would always kick me out.

One of my favorite places to hang out was in my own back yard. We had lived in this house since I was five years old. It was actually built for us. The yard was a good size, about a half acre. The back end of the yard was not finished off or landscaped. Most of it consisted of tall, uncut grass. But, in one section, just behind the lawn was a collection of trees that had been cut down but not hauled away.

These were "the logs."

The logs consisted of about five tree trunks and huge branches. Toward the back was a fallen tree trunk about ten feet long and two or three feet wide. One end was cut evenly, but the other end had the stub of a severed branch sticking up. This log was usually known as the elephant. This served as an excellent elephant whenever we played Jungle Jim. It also doubled as a submarine, jet plane, helicopter, horse, car, tank or even Moby Dick.

Three huge branches, each about ten inches in diameter, were laying in the form of a triangle. They made a great boat, or a raft, or a tank or bunker, or even a space ship. The ground was slightly dug out in the center of the triangle, so you could hunker down and not be seen. These logs were usually known as the boat.

My favorite of all was another tree trunk that was about two feet in diameter. The tree originally had a large, thick branch, which had been severed, but the stump resembled a horse's neck. The trunk was the right size for the body. This was *my* log. My log was my horse (any number of cowboys: Paladin, Roy Rogers, Lone Ranger, etc.), elephant (Circus Boy, Jungle Jim), car (Johnny Jet), submarine, camel, jet plane (Steve Canyon), helicopter (Whirlybirds), train engine (Casey Jones), or anything else I needed it to be. Sometimes I would use an "Indian" blanket as a saddle. I could sit on my log for hours and pretend.

This Sunday, as I sat on "Silver" looking for outlaws, I saw Doug walking out of his back door. He seemed to have a slight limp. At least, he wasn't walking normally.

"What happened to you?" I asked as he approached.

Doug's face was contorted. He was obviously in some kind of pain. Reaching his right hand around to his backside, he rubbed his right buttock. Then he replied in a mock Scottish accent.

"Ah kenna sit doon. Muh fatherrr hit me in a soft spot!"

"What are you talking about?" I asked.

"That's Scottish," he answered. "I can't sit down. My father hit me in a soft spot - you know, my butt!

"What happened?"

"After Mass today I was in the garage and I tried smoking a cigarette that I snitched from my father. He caught me smoking it and smacked me in the rear. Boy, did that hurt!"

I chuckled. It was kind of funny that he got spanked. Doug was a year older than I. He was also taller.

"Why would you even try smoking?" I asked. "It's so gross and disgusting!"

"I just thought I'd try. I didn't like it, though. You're right. It was gross with a capital G!"

We both laughed and started gagging.

"I would never try it," I offered, as we both sat down in the boat logs. "My parents both smoke a lot. And my father...ugh! When he wakes up in the morning I can always hear this *hack! hack! hack! wuff!*" I made a series of disgusting coughing sounds."Then, the next thing I hear is the *click* of his Zippo lighter as he lights up a cigarette!"

We both started hacking and coughing, laughing so hard that we fell on top of each other. Our throats were raw from making all that noise and we were totally out of breath.

"And of course, there's also Mr. Gregory, my sixth grade teacher. I didn't know until someone told me that he's a chain smoker. But, every now and then he'd come over to my desk, and bend over me to say something or look at something I was doing...and the stink would almost knock me out!"

More gagging!

"I used to think, 'If *that's* what it smells like to be a man, I don't want to *ever* grow up!'"

More coughing, gagging and holding our noses!

"Then I found out he was a chain smoker. No way am I ever gonna put a butt in *my* mouth! Gaaaa-ross!"

Suddenly, Doug got up, turned his back to me and stuck his rear end in my face!

"Now you have a butt in your mouth!" he laughed. I pushed him away.

"Oh, gross! *Plah! Plah! Plah!*" I spat.

We laughed uncontrollably for a few minutes. Then, I got a sudden urge. I took an imaginary glove and swung it at his face.

"*Doosh! Doosh! Doosh!* Lt. Beamish, I challenge you to a duel for sticking your butt in my face," I stated. We used to play *The Buccaneer* all the time. It was one of my favorite games based on a TV series. I was Captain Dan Tempest, a pirate, and Doug was Lt. Beamish, Acting Governor of New Providence. "Choose your weapon. Swords or pistols!"

"Lt. Beamish" quickly sprang to his feet and looked around for suitable weapons.

"Why swords, of course, Captain Tempest!" he answered.

We each looked around in the grass to find stout sticks that would make good swords. Quickly we found our weapons, cleared them, as best we could, of little branches and leaves. We stood in our positions, saluted each other.

"On guard!" I said. Suddenly, we began slashing and whipping our swords at each other. Neither of us was very good at swordplay, but we both thought we were experts. We jumped from log to log. Lunged, parried, swung. We both made sound effects as we attacked. Finally, with a forceful lunge, my opponent stuck me straight in the chest. Although the sword bent and snapped, I wasn't really hurt. But, I feigned a mortal wound.

"Ah! Oh! Uh! Uh! Eeee! Ah!" I writhed in pain and agony.

Doug crossed his arms, did his best to look fierce, and said, "Tempest, will you just shut up and die?"

"Ah, Oooo! Eeeee! I thought you were my friend. Oh, what a tangled web we weave, when first we practice to deceive," I moaned. Then, in an aside I said, "Shakespeare!"

"Shakespeare?" my friend blurted. "Dan Tempest doesn't quote Shakespeare!"

"No," I responded. "But Paladin does."

"I thought you were Dan Tempest."

"I am, but I think it's cool when Paladin quotes Shakespeare. So, I thought I'd do it as Dan Tempest," I explained. We both immediately discarded our swords and sat back down on the side of the boat.

"Paladin is pretty cool," agreed Doug.

"He's the best," I said.

Playing pirates, cops and robbers, cowboys and Indians and other games like that had always been fun. Doug and I let our imaginations run wild. But, we were beginning to realize that we were older now, and those games would soon just be a part of our past - fond memories. He had just finished his first year in junior high, and I had finished my last year in elementary school. Life was changing for us both.

On Wednesday, Doug and I stood at the bus stop waiting to go to Quincy Square to see the new movie *Journey to the Center of the Earth*. We had seen commercials about this film and were very excited about seeing it. Pat Boone was supposed to be in it. We knew he was a popular singer, but we didn't know that he could act.

What a movie! Based on Jules Verne's book, this sci-fi film

chronicles the expedition of Sir Oliver Lindenbrook (James Mason) and his young assistant Alec (Pat Boone) to follow in the footsteps of explorer Arne Saknussem to the center of the earth's core. The explorers begin their journey by going into an extinct volcano in Iceland. Members of the expedition include Sir Oliver, Alec, the widow of another explorer, and an Icelandic guide Hans, accompanied by his pet duck Gertrude. They are followed by the evil Count Saknussem. A lot of this movie was filmed in the Carlsbad Caverns in New Mexico, so it was very spectacular.

The group not only finds the center of the earth, but also stumbles across the sunken city of Atlantis. They return to the surface via another volcano using some of the worst special effects ever filmed. Little dolls in a bowl! But, that scene didn't stop me from being total, awesomely inspired by the movie.

"Hey, Doug," I said on the bus as we rode home. "I think we should go on a journey to the center of the earth."

"How are we going to get there?" was his first question.

"Caves, of course," I answered. My plan was to find some local caves and use them as a starting point, because there were no volcanos nearby and our allowances wouldn't take us to Iceland.

This would all require a great deal of research. So, this meant another trip to the library. There, I took out books on geology, speleology (the study of caves), and spelunking (cave exploring). Within a few days, I was drawing diagrams of volcanoes and cross sections of planet earth. I discovered that there was a crust, mantel and core. In short, I became an overnight "expert" on the subjects. Of course, I also took out a copy of the original Jules Verne novel, **Journey to the Center of the Earth**.

Doug and I also had to plan for our own expedition. The first thing that we needed to do was make a list of everything we would need to take on our journey: Rope, flashlights, extra batteries, water, dehydrated food, cookies, oatmeal, sleeping bags, clothing, toilet paper....the list went on and on.

After making several inquiries at the library and by telephone, I wasn't able to come up with the location of any caves in our area. I was also told by most sources that cave exploring was "very dangerous" and should only be attempted by experts. Of course, after all the reading that I had done, I considered myself well qualified. But, when I wasn't able to locate any caves, I was undaunted. I would dig my own! There was plenty of room in the tall grass in my back yard. So, I began to dig. I located a good area behind the incinerator, marked off a space about four feet square, and using one of my father's shovels and a pitchfork, Doug and I began our excavation.

Almost every day, I would get the shovel and pitchfork from the shed and go out to the back yard to dig a little. Although this was hard work, it wasn't like doing the chores that I was assigned by my parents. This was a scientific expedition. Besides, even if I didn't take a journey to the center of the earth, at least I could dig a cave that I could use like a secret hideout, my own lair. Maybe even a secret laboratory where I could do experiments like the mad scientists in all those movies I watched on Saturday morning and afternoon TV. As I wielded the shovel, I would imagine all sorts of possibilities for my cave.

Chapter Four

My favorite hobby was magic. I was hooked when my parents went to some kind of adult party where everyone got a gag gift, and my father happened to get a *Sneaky Pete Magic Set*. He spent a little bit of time learning the simple tricks, then after supper one night, he decided to show off.

Pa did a card trick where he had my sister pick a card, then he held it in his hand with the face side away from him, so that he wasn't able to see it. Then, he magically named the card! We were all amazed. I even tried to explain it by describing how the name of the card somehow ran through his arm and up to his brain. Moments later, he revealed that the secret was simply a small mirror that he had hidden in the palm of his hand. He could see the reflection, but we couldn't see the mirror.

From that point on, I wanted to learn everything I could about magic. The library was the main source of my information. From time to time there would be a magician on television, usually on *The Ed Sullivan Show* or *Hollywood Palace*. When that happened, I was in my glory, glued to the TV. By the time I was eleven I had made and/or bought enough tricks to put on a show. In an attempt to make some cash that summer, I had placed a small classified ad in the local newspaper: *Harry Voldini, the Teenage Conjuror will present magic shows for children's parties. Call VI 3-5783.*

Harry Voldini was my stage name. Having read a biography of Harry Houdini, I knew that sometimes magicians didn't use their own names, but created new ones which were often formed from the names of magicians whom they admired. So, I adopted 'Harry' from Houdini's name. 'Voldini' came from the name of a fictitious magician character whom I saw on television in an old Humphrey Bogart movie. I wasn't quite a teenager yet, but I thought that sounded better than Harry Voldini, Not-quite Teenage Magician.

One weeknight, my parents were entertaining a few friends, our neighbor, Marion, and my father's friend, Dave. Marion was the neighborhood gossip. Dave was one of my father's National Guard buddies. He was tall, heavy-set and sported a thick mustache that matched his mop of black hair. I liked Dave. Even though he was about ten years younger than my father, sometimes he acted like a kid. When he got excited, he would smile real big and his eyes would get wide. He even giggled when he laughed.

The grown-ups were all talking about grown-up stuff as I listened in. Donna was in the other room watching TV. The telephone in my parent's bedroom began to ring. Being the closest, I ran to answer it.

"Hello," I said.

"Hello," responded a woman. "May I speak with Harry Voldini?"

"That's me!"

"Oh, good. I'm having a birthday party for my eight year-old son next week and I wondered if you were available and how much you charge."

A rush of excitement ran through my whole body. I was tingling! Someone actually read my ad and wanted me to do a show!

"Well, when is the party?"

"Friday at 7 o'clock."

"Okay, well, I charge five dollars for a half hour, but I can also do a one hour show for ten dollars."

I wondered if she would think the price was too high.

"That's very reasonable."

I took down all the necessary information about location and time, then hung up. Beaming, I walked back into the kitchen and made my announcement.

"I have a magic show next Friday night in Weymouth and I'm making ten dollars."

Eyebrows raised and there were some smiles, especially from Dave.

"Congratulations!" he said.

Then, my father asked, "How are you going to get there?"

My heart sank. I just assumed that my mother or father would be gracious enough to drive me. The thought of them not doing so never entered my mind. Was my father saying that no one was going to take me?

"I thought...one of you would," I said hesitantly.

Pa just raised his left eyebrow and said, "Oh."

Dave seemed to sense my dilemma and he spoke up.

"I'll take you! Sounds like fun."

Dave was very supportive. He was almost as excited about this as I was. But, I was disappointed that my father didn't seem to share our enthusiasm. I was puzzled. Why didn't he make some kind of positive remark or give me some words of encouragement? Why did that have to come from someone else?

When I went to bed that night, I remembered a trip that I had taken that past winter with Pa and Dave. My father liked to go deer hunting every winter. He would go once or twice on weekends. One time, my mother talked him into taking me with him. Neither Pa nor I were quite sure what I would be doing while he was hunting, so I brought along a few magic tricks and books.

Dave's family had a house in the woods in New Hampshire. They called it a farm, although there were no animals. As we drove to New Hampshire, we stopped at several gun shops so the two hunters could look at the latest weapons. At one point, as they were browsing, Dave looked at me and noticed that I wasn't really looking at the guns.

"Gee," he said. "We've stopped at some gun shops, but maybe we should stop at a magic shop on the way up."

"Thanks," I said. "But I don't think there are any between here and New Hampshire." I really appreciated Dave's thoughtfulness. I'm sure the idea had never occurred to Pa.

Anyway, that Friday following the phone call, Dave came to our house at about 6 o'clock to pick me up. My father went along for the ride. My first "professional" magic show...I got paid ten dollars and even received a five dollar tip!

I took my money and invested it in a brown, imitation leather attache case that I could use to store my magic tricks and to look more professional when I went to do a show. But, I decided that a plain brown case wasn't professional enough, so I asked my father if he would paint my stage name on the top lid of the case. He took it to work with him. Several days later he brought it back home. I had expected to see my name in plain block letters, but, instead Pa had created a logo for me. The words "The Amazing" went straight across the top, but "Voldini" was beneath the first line, angled up at about 45 degrees and in script. The whole thing was done in gold leaf. I was amazed for sure.

"Thanks," I said. "It looks great!"

"Take good care of it," was his only response.

Monday morning, I was sitting on Trigger, gently caressing his mane, when Doug came running out of his back door.

"Hey, Eddy!" he called. "My Dad's taking the day off from work and he said he'd take my sister and brothers and me to the 'Y' to go swimming. I asked him if you could come and he said it'd be okay. Go get your suit!"

I wanted to go with my friend, but I knew that I had to beg off.

"Thanks," I said, not looking him in the eye. "But, I can't go today. I have an ear infection, so I'm not allowed to go in the water."

"Okay, have it your way. Maybe next time. See you this after!" He ran back home.

Of course, I was lying. No ear infection. The truth was that I was embarrassed to admit that I couldn't swim. My sister had taken to the water like a fish when we were younger, but I was a little hesitant. I wasn't quite sure of the water.

Pa would sometimes try to help me. He would go out into the water a little way, then beckon me to join him.

"Come on out," he would say. "There's nothing to be afraid of. I'll hold you up. Trust me."

When I expressed my reticence, he would counter with, "Don't be a chicken!" Unfortunately, he didn't realize that he was sending me lots of mixed messages. "There's nothing to be afraid of" said that I *was* afraid of something. "Don't be a chicken" said that he thought I *was* a chicken, but shouldn't be that way. So my father was telling me that there was something to be afraid of and that I was a chicken. After all, he was older and wiser, so he must have known what he was talking about.

But, the biggest mixed message was when he said "Trust me." He had told me before about how he learned to swim.

"When I was your age, I learned to swim when my father picked me up and threw me into the water. I had to swim or drown. So, I swam."

Well, how was I to know if my father would or wouldn't replicate his own father's actions and throw *me* into the water!?!?!?! That was one of my biggest fears. And when Pa would come after me to try to pick me up and take me into the water, that was enough to send me into a fit of crying. He never should have told me that story.

Swimming wasn't the only situation that caused me embarrassment. Sometimes Doug wanted to ride bikes. I needed an excuse for that one, too. Yes, I had a bicycle, but I couldn't ride it.

One Christmas, Donna and I both got bicycles. This was great! When the weather was warmer we would have a chance to go outside and learn to ride them. Just like with the water, my sister had perfect balance and learned to ride her bike immediately. I was a different story. Once again, I was hesitant and had a little trouble getting my balance.

"Can I have training wheels?" I had asked.

Pa rolled his eyes up into his head and sighed.

"Training wheels are for sissies. No son of mine is going to use training wheels. Trust me. I'll hold you while you learn to balance."

There was that "trust me" again. The phrase didn't inspire a lot of confidence. Was he going to hold me and then let me go? Sure enough, that's what he did. I fell several times. What also didn't help much was that we were practicing on the grass in the back yard. No slope at all. Just level ground. I couldn't get my balance. There was no momentum. Very quickly, I became discouraged. That was probably the only time we ever tried it. The bike went into the cellar and gathered dust.

There were many times that I wished I could ride that bike. I saw other kids riding them. Jeff on *Lassie* rode his. Riding my tricycle had been lots of fun, so I could only imagine that riding a two-wheeler would be even more fun. The rush of the wind in your face. It was just like riding a horse or a motorcycle. What a feeling of freedom there must be. But, I was not to experience these wonderful feelings. When Doug would ask me to go bike riding, I would make up some excuse. My tires were flat. Something was out of line. It was just plain broken. Eventually he stopped asking me to ride bikes. Besides, walking was good exercise.

The following day found Doug and me sitting under the pig nut tree. We were lying down on our stomachs, arm wrestling. It wasn't really much of a contest, because Doug was stronger than I was, but I was determined to try to win.

"Aren't you ready to quit yet?" my friend asked.

"Just one more time," I sighed. My arm was aching, but I wanted to give it one last try.

"Are you two girls makin' out?" came a loud voice from not too far away. We both jumped because we were startled. But, I quickly managed to pin Doug's arm to the ground. We looked up and saw Jimmy Campbell. He was the same age as Douglas, but taller, with very dark hair, bushy eyebrows and the hint of a mustache on his top lip. We both dreaded his appearance.

"Oh, shut up, Campbell!" was Doug's response.

"Hmph! Make me, Collier!"

Jimmy was not very well-liked. He was loud and overbearing. He had a reputation for getting into trouble and for being a bully.

"Is Dracula sucking your blood?" Jimmy sarcastically asked.

He was referring to the previous Halloween. I had been dressed as Dracula and Jimmy was the Frankenstein monster. For some reason, he and I had gone trick or treating together. I think Doug was sick or something, and there was no one else around to go with. So, I went with Jimmy, much to my mother's dismay. She didn't like him at all.

"He's a troublemaker, and besides he's older than you," she had said.

Anyway, I liked to scare the little kids by holding my arms up under my cape, as though I had bat wings, growling at them and showing my plastic fangs. But, Jimmy would chase them and growl very loudly until some of them screamed and cried. One time, a couple of kids were so scared that they dropped their bags. Jimmy just scooped up their candy and put it in his own bag. I didn't think that was very nice.

I didn't mind his Dracula remark, but Doug got angry. He stood up and walked toward Jimmy. His face was turning red and his fists were clenched.

"Shut the hell up, Campbell!"

"Gonna make me?" was his goading reply.

Douglas took a deep breath, stretched his fingers and shook his head. Then he mumbled, "Aw, your mother wears combat boots."

Jimmy's face reddened and his eyes widened.

"What did you say about my mother?" he asked, talking through his clenched teeth.

"...and she smokes like a chimney," Doug continued.

I could feel my body getting tense as I started to stand up. I didn't like where this was going. This could break out into a fight at any minute, and I knew that Jimmy would probably win because he was taller and bigger than Doug.

Jimmy's eyes began to narrow and I could see that he was clenching his right fist, drawing his arm back just slightly. His chest was widening as he inhaled deeply.

"And your old man's a drunk!" was Doug's final blow.

Jimmy Campbell's mouth opened, and the air just slowly hissed from between his lips. His shoulders slumped as he opened his fist. He closed his eyes and turned around abruptly. As he began walking away, we could hear, "You son of a...."

Chapter Five

Sunday morning at breakfast my mother announced that the following week we would be driving to New Hampshire for a family vacation.

"Oh, no!" groaned my sister. Donna was at that age when young people don't want to have anything to do with their parents, if they can help it - let alone go on vacation with them. After all, she was fifteen years old and she had girlfriends and boyfriends that she wanted to hang out with.

Mom continued. "Your father has been planning this for a long time and he really wants us to do it. It could be a lot of fun. We realize that this may be the last family vacation we take together. You kids are growing up."

"Where are we going in New Hampshire?" I asked.

"We're going to spend a week at the Double A Dude Ranch."

"A dude ranch!?!?!?" Donna shrieked.

I thought it sounded like it might be rather cool. After all, Pa and I liked cowboys. And my impression of a dude ranch was that it would be like the Triple R Ranch on the Disney series *Spin and Marty*. So, I was okay with the whole idea, even though I wasn't totally thrilled.

Pa sat there and said nothing. Mom did all the talking, which was usual. She was the real organizer.

"So, I want you to think about packing your suitcases. I'll let you know what kind of clothes to bring."

"And your mother will supervise," added Pa.

When we packed that next week, I made sure to bring along a few magic tricks to practice. Some cards and a few silk handkerchiefs.

We arrived at the Double A Dude Ranch on the following Sunday afternoon. As we drove up to the main entrance, we could all see that it was a little run-down. The ranch was surrounded by a tall, white corral-type fence. Over the gate were two big "A"s, superimposed over each other. Below them were the words "Dude Ranch." The weeds around the fence were overgrown, and the paint was chipped quite a bit. The fence hadn't been painted in quite some time. Although the driveway was paved, it had plenty of cracks that were filling up with grass and weeds.

"Oh, great," mumbled my sister.

"Just be quiet," responded my mother. "I'm sure it's going to be fine."

Donna would spend the whole week with a scowl on her face and her arms crossed. She was not at all thrilled to be there. Definitely not cool.

When we drove up to the main ranch house, we were greeted by a young man in western attire. He welcomed us in a put-on southern accent with a great big "Howdy, folks!" After my parents signed us in, we drove to a small cabin not far from the main building. This is where we would live for the next six days.

After unpacking and settling in, we got dressed to go to dinner. This took place in the main building. Each family was assigned a table and a particular waitress for their entire stay. Our waitress was Beth. She was a college student from New Hampshire, very pleasant, well mannered, and well endowed, which my father quickly noticed. After Beth took our order and went off to the kitchen, Pa made a gesture with his hands in front of his chest, nodded toward Beth and said to my mother, "I wonder if they're real." She just shook her head. He had a "naughty" streak in him.

Monday was the Fourth of July, so we went into town to see the parade. It was very comical. The high school marching band started it off, followed by homemade floats by local merchants, including Joe's Septic Service. That one got a laugh. Later into the parade was a big, white Cadillac convertible with Al Andrews, the "cowboy" who owned the Double A Dude Ranch. He was accompanied by several pretty young women in gowns. The whole parade seemed to take about ten minutes.

After lunch we went to the tennis courts. I had begun to learn how to play tennis, so I did fairly well. The tennis court, however, was in poor shape. The asphalt was cracked and had weeds and grass growing here and there. The nets were broken and we had to fix them before we could play. There were four courts. The one opposite us was the only other one in use. There was another mother, father, sister, brother group. The sister was blond and looked to be about my age. The brother was probably seven or eight. At one point, my mother approached me, nodded toward the blond girl and said, "Why don't you go ask her to play?" But, my self-confidence and social skills were not ready for that!

After dinner we were treated to a variety show. This got me

excited. There were a few singers, dancers, an acrobatic husband and wife team, a comedian and a magician. The comedian did not appeal to me. I didn't think he was very funny. Most of his material was composed of off-color jokes, which my mother would refer to as "dirty jokes." I didn't understand most of them, and the ones that I did understand I found offensive and embarrassing. My father thought he was hilarious. My mother laughed sometimes, but other times looked embarrassed, too. My sister understood more of the jokes than I did, but even she looked uncomfortable.

The magician was a different story altogether. He was fantastic. I had even seen him on the *Ed Sullivan Show*. His name was Korengo. He did tricks with doves, silks, coins and cards, then climaxed his act with Houdini's trademark illusion known as *Metamorphosis* or the *Substitution Trunk*. His wife handcuffed him, tied him in a cloth bag, then put him in a round trunk which she padlocked. She jumped on top of the trunk and pulled up a big cloth tube that covered her and the trunk. She yelled, "One! Two!" then lowered the cloth tube and Korengo appeared in her place as he yelled, "Three!" He jumped down from the trunk, unlocked it, untied the bag and there was his wife, handcuffed just as he had been. Spectacular!

They were the final act. The MC, the Social Director named Jim, announced that on Friday night we would have a talent show featuring staff and guests, so anyone who had a talent that they would like to share was welcome to let him know. I knew what I was going to do!

I had enough courage to go back stage after the show and introduce myself to Korengo and his wife. I told them how much I had enjoyed their performance and that I was an amateur magician myself. They wished me luck.

Tuesday, Wednesday and Thursday we went horseback riding, played more tennis and did some local sightseeing. The first two nights guests were treated to a movie. Thursday night we had a dance. Members of the staff were available to dance with guests. Of course, Pa took this opportunity to dance with our waitress, Beth. Before he asked her, he turned to my mother and said, "Now I'll find out if they're real!" He danced a waltz with her, then returned to our table and announced, "They're real!"

On and off during the week, I took time to prepare for my magic act. I decided to do only two tricks. The first would be a torn and restored newspaper trick and the second would be my version of the dancing handkerchief. There was a brief rehearsal with the band on Friday morning. I was ready to go. Fortunately, my mother had thought to have me pack a suit.

I waited anxiously in the wings. This was the first time that I would be performing in front of a large audience, so I was a little nervous. But, my props were ready and so was I. The stage manager told me to take my place. I was introduced as Voldini, the Lazy Magician. The reason for the title was that I had decided to do my act sitting in a chair. I had heard about a famous magician named Dante who did a part of his show seated, and called it the Lazy Magician, so I thought I'd give this a try.

Sitting in the chair, legs crossed, reading my newspaper, I waited for the curtain to open. The audience applauded politely when they heard the introduction. The curtains parted. For several seconds I ignored the audience as I continued to read the paper. I acted startled, as though I had just realized that the audience was there.

"Oops! Sorry, I was just reading my newspaper," I said. I tore the large sheet of newspaper down the center, folded it in two and tore it again. I tore the paper a third and fourth time. Then, as I was about to discard the newspaper, I pretended to be interested in an article. As I gave the paper a shake, it opened out fully restored! Wow! The applause was great! I had taken them by surprise. I nodded in appreciation and extended my hands.

I raised my right index finger as though to say, "Wait a minute" as the band began to play the music I had requested, *Funny Talk* from Bert Kaemfert's album *Dancing in Wonderland* - one of my favorites. Reaching into my jacket breast pocket, I removed my red silk handkerchief, tied a knot in one end, then placed it on the floor. I motioned my hands in time to the music a few times, then the silk came to life. It jumped up and began to dance. First it danced in the middle, between my feet, then it jumped to one side for a few beats, then to the other for a few more beats. Back and forth, back and forth, several times until the music reached a climax, at which point the silk jumped up into the air, then dropped to the stage. I stood up, bowed and received a thunderous round of applause. At least, it seemed thunderous to me! In the front row, I saw the blond girl with her family. She was smiling up at me, looking thoroughly impressed. I wished that I had had an opportunity to do this performance earlier in the week. Maybe she would have played tennis with me!

When I rejoined my family I was met with a variety of

responses.

"You did a very good job, Eddy," said my mother.

My father just smiled. My sister gave me a sarcastic-looking smile that said, "Big deal." Nonetheless, I was thrilled with the experience.

The next morning, after packing, as we were preparing to leave, we stopped in the gift shop to buy a few snacks and souvenirs. The blond girl's mother approached me.

"You're the boy who did the magic show last night aren't you?" she asked.

"Yes, I am," I replied.

"Well, my daughter's a little shy, but she wanted me to tell you that she thought you did a marvelous job. In fact, we all thought you did great. We didn't know you were a magician."

The blond girl was about ten feet away from her mother. I looked at her, smiled and said "Thank you very much" to her mother. Wish she had told me herself!

Chapter Six

The following Monday, Douglas and I walked up the street to hang out at our favorite spot.

"So, Doug," I said as we walked, "what's junior high like?"

"It's okay," he answered. "Instead of just having one teacher and staying in one room all day, you have a different teacher and a different room for every subject."

"Wow! So, how many teachers do you have?"

"Well, there's seven periods every day. A period is almost an hour long, so you have at least seven different teachers."

"How do you know what classes you have and what teachers to go to?"

"At the beginning of the year, you get a schedule. That tells what subjects you have every day, what rooms, what times, what teachers."

"But, how do you remember all that?" I was confused already.

"You write it down and keep it with you."

"Do you have your own desk?" I asked.

"You have a different desk in every classroom."

"But, where do you keep all your stuff?"

"You get a locker outside your homeroom class."

"Homeroom? What's that?" I asked.

"That's where you start every day. They take attendance and you goof off for a while. They have announcements, then you go to your classes."

"Tell me about the lockers." This idea excited me.

"Well, you have a locker. The locker has a number. Your name's not on it. Just the number. You keep your books in there, your lunch, your jacket and stuff."

"Can't other kids steal your stuff?" was my next question.

"No, the locker has a combination lock, like a safe. You have to memorize it so no one else can open it."

Now, this sounded a little scary.

"But, what if you forget the combination?"

"No sweat. The teachers have keys. But, you have another locker, too. A gym locker. You have to remember that combination, too."

Two combinations! That was going to be too much.

"What do ya need a gym locker for?" I asked.

"When you have gym you have to wear a gym uniform...shorts and a t-shirt. So, you change in the boys' locker room and leave your regular clothes and your books in the locker while you have gym."

Now wait a minute.

"You change clothes...?"

"That's right."

"In the locker room?"

"Yuh huh."

"In front of everybody?"

"Yuh, so what?" Doug had two brothers, one older and one younger, so this was no big deal to him, but I only had an older sister and wasn't used to changing in front of anyone else. "And then when gym's over, you take a shower and go to your next class."

Oh, great!

"You take a shower?"

"That's right," replied the voice of experience. "They have this one big shower room where everybody takes a shower together."

"Together?" This was sounding even worse.

"Yup, together."

"*Naked?*"

"Naked," Doug said with another of those *so what* looks on his face. "But you don't look. Nobody looks at anybody else."

I was so modest about my body that I usually wore a t-shirt when I went swimming. Besides, I had begun to mature early. My voice had already changed and I was sprouting hair in new places. In fact, I had already begun to shave my upper lip once a week. Now, I was told that I was going to be totally naked in front of a whole mess of other guys! Maybe I could skip gym somehow.

"Don't sweat it," Doug advised. "It's no big deal."

Well, maybe no big deal to him, but to Mr. Modest over here it was a *very* big deal.

Once we saw the pig nut tree in the distance, we both began to run. It was never a fair race with Doug. He was taller and had longer legs. Of course, he beat me. We leaned against the tree and tried to catch our breath. I gazed out at the distance. It was quite a view. But, as

I spotted Fore River Ship Yard, I began to get a sense of dread. I was remembering a conversation that we had in class just before the end of school. The sadness and fear crept over me. I just continued to stare out at the ship yard.

"Doug," I said quietly. "Do you think the Russians'll ever drop the bomb on us?"

"You mean World War III?"

"Yeah."

"I dunno." He became very serious, too. "A couple of months ago, I saw this show on *Playhouse 90*. It was about what would happen if we did have a World War III."

I just listened quietly.

"There was this one scene where a bunch of people were having a party or something after the Russians started dropping bombs. One old lady was complaining that she was having trouble getting her medicine. She said that her doctor told her it'd be coming soon. They had to ship it in from somewhere else. This other guy asked her where it was coming from. She told him it was coming from Florida. The guy just looked at her for awhile, then he said, 'There is no Florida'."

A chill ran up my spine, and my scalp tingled.

"Yeah," I sighed. "Before school was out, we were practicing 'duck and cover' one day, when some kid asked Mr. Gregory about the bomb. We had all heard that if you were far away from a bomb you'd still be killed by radiation poisoning, and that might take a long time."

"That's right," added Doug. "Your skin rots and your flesh falls off! You puke all over the place."

"Then, another kid asked what Mr. Gregory thought would happen to *us* once they started bombing," I continued. "I don't think he wanted to answer the question, cuz he was very quiet for a long time. Then he explained that the Russians would hit military targets first, like air bases, military bases, supply depots, and places where they make tanks, ammunition and ships.

"Mr. Gregory got this funny look on his face, and then he told us that Fore River Ship Yard is only a few miles away from us..." As I said this, I stared across the grassy field and at the ship yard in the distance and my scalp tingled even more. I was scaring myself. "...and that would be a military target. He said it'd happen so fast that we wouldn't know what hit us. We'd all be gone. We wouldn't have to worry about radiation poisoning."

We were both very quiet and still for a long time. Just the

thought that we could be here today and gone tomorrow was enough to make us stop. We didn't think about anything in particular. It was more like our minds were just frozen. We *couldn't* think about anything in particular. We just couldn't think. We couldn't imagine what it would be like. We didn't even *want* to imagine what it might be like.

Doug broke the silence.

"My daddy works at the ship yard," he said.

"What?"

"Say, 'My daddy works at the ship yard'."

"I know this one," I replied.

"Just do it!" said Doug. He could be very persuasive sometimes.

"Okay. My daddy works at the ship yard."

"Now, stick out your tongue, hold onto it and say it again."

I knew what was coming, but I did it anyway. This time the word 'ship' came out differently. Doug laughed. He stuck out his own tongue, held onto it and said the phrase. We both laughed. We looked at each other, held our tongues and repeated "My daddy works at the ship yard" about ten times. That was stupid, but it was fun. And it helped us shift gears.

We both sat down under the tree.

"How come you didn't go out for Little League?" asked Doug. "I thought you liked baseball."

"Naw, not any more. I didn't go out for it last summer either."

"Why not?"

"Well, I used to like it, but I stink at it. I can't catch good. I usually strike out. So, no one wants me on their team. I really wanted to be a catcher, but they wouldn't let me, even when my father helped coach the team. The coach just kept saying 'We'll see' and you know what 'We'll see' means."

"Yup," replied Doug. "It means you'll *never* see!"

"That's right," I agreed. "They always used to put me way out in the outfield. Well, the last game of the season, my parents, my sister, my favorite aunt and uncle all came to watch the game. I was way out in left field and I had no idea what was going on. I was just kicking rocks. All of a sudden, everyone starts yelling and screaming at me! The ball was coming to me. It was a grounder...and I missed it."

Doug couldn't help but laugh. *No one* misses a grounder when you're way out in left field.

"So, I ran after it and got it. By the time I had it, I had no idea what was going on. I looked toward home and everyone was yelling at me to throw it to them...the pitcher, the catcher, all the basemen. I didn't know what the heck to do!"

Doug started to laugh real hard. I couldn't blame him, although it wasn't very funny to me at the time it happened.

"So, I just kinda threw it in the direction of home. When I looked over my shoulder, I saw my mother, father, sister, aunt and uncle all laughing at me. It was embarrassing."

By this time, Doug was rolling on the ground, holding his sides.

"Thanks a pant-load!" I said.

He held his sides, then he held his hand over his mouth. Soon he was coughing and choking. After a few moments, Doug finally calmed down.

"Boy, I'm sorry, but that was funny."

"Yeah, I guess it is now," I said. "But, when it happened, I didn't think so. After that, I quit Little League. That was enough for me."

As Doug sat back up, he stared at my face for a minute, and scrunched his eyebrows.

"What?" I asked.

"How long have you been wearin' glasses?" he asked.

"Since the beginning of fifth grade," I answered. "Why?"

He still had that look on his face.

"Why'd you start wearin' them?"

"Oh," I began. "That's another story. At the end of fourth grade, Miss Phelan put a whole bunch of arithmetic examples on the blackboards. We were supposed to copy them, figure them out, then pass 'em in. Well, I did. The next day, when she passed them back, I got a big fat 'F' on my paper."

"How come?"

"She said, in front of the whole class, that I was a cheater. 'Edward,' she said, 'You cheated on this paper, so I gave you an F.' But, I didn't cheat and I told her I didn't. Then she says, 'Yes, you did. You didn't like the examples I put on the board, so you wrote your own. And even though you got most of them correct, you cheated, so you deserve a failing grade!'

"But, I really didn't cheat. I couldn't see the examples very good, so I squinted and copied them the best I could. So, later on, after I went to the eye doctor's, it turned out that I'm near-sighted. I couldn't see the examples well enough to copy them right. I thought they were right, but some threes looked like eights, and all that stuff. And Mrs. Phelan never told the class I didn't cheat and she never apologized."

"Grown-ups never apologize," Doug added.

"I guess you're right. Then my father says to me that the reason I have to wear glasses is because I read too many books. And my mother says it's because I sit too close to the TV. My father wasn't happy that I had to wear glasses. He even called me 'four eyes'."

"I think you kinda look like Clark Kent," was Doug's response.

"I wish I *was* Clark Kent. So, why'd you want to know how long I've been wearing glasses?"

"When'd you stop Little League?"

"I guess it was that summer, between fourth and fifth grade." Doug scratched his chin, then his head.

"Well, I figure that maybe the reason you didn't do so well in baseball was 'cuz you couldn't *see* the ball. Not 'cuz you're not good at it. But just 'cuz you couldn't see the ball good enough to catch it or hit it."

It was like a light turned on in my head. Douglas was right! He was pretty smart. That actually made me feel a lot better. I had thought that I was clumsy. Now I realized that maybe I wasn't. I just had bad eyes. But, I still felt vulnerable. Kids who wear glasses can't do a lot of things that other kids can, because maybe their glasses will get knocked off and broken. I thought about that a lot. And how many cool people wore glasses? None! Paladin, Yancy Derringer, Roy Rogers, Captain Midnight, Captain Marvel. None of those guys wore glasses. The only one who did was Superman, but that was only when he was Clark Kent. Bummer!

Chapter Seven

July thirteenth marked my twelfth birthday. Surely this would be a great day for me. A crossroads. A step toward adulthood. I was out of elementary school and would be going to junior high in September. This was a momentous occasion for me. No big party, but at least a cake (maybe a chocolate devil's food cake with chocolate frosting) and a small Schultz family gathering. I was getting too old for birthday parties anyway.

BUT...Pa was away for two weeks going to National Guard camp. Donna was spending a few days in Cape Cod with her girlfriend Carol. At least that left me with Mom. BUT...it was a Wednesday, and Wednesday was my mother's Bridge Club night. She *seemed* sincere when she said that she was sorry, but she had to go. The girls were counting on her. She had a kind of crooked, embarrassed smile when she told me this.

So, I celebrated my twelfth birthday alone. Alone, except for my stupid "surrogate brother" dog Laddie. We sat at the kitchen table together. I put him on a chair so he could sit next to me. Together we sang "Happy Birthday to me." And life went on.

Even though Pa wasn't there for my actual birthday, he did have a present for me when he came home from National Guard. He always brought me and my sister a small gift, like a t-shirt, when he went away. This time he had two wrapped gifts. One was about three feet long and the other about four feet. I couldn't imagine what they might be. I tore open the paper that covered the largest. It was a real bow and arrows! Shades of Robin Hood! I loved my Dad! What a gift!

"You have to be real careful with this," he cautioned. "And you can only use it with supervision. Never alone. You use it *once* alone and it's gone forever. You hear me?"

"Yes! Yes! That's okay. Supervision is great!"

I was not about to lose the chance to use a *real* bow and arrow. For years I had used my jackknife to cut down branches, tie some string to the ends and make these weak little bows that barely shot my crooked arrows a few feet. But, now I had the real thing.

If this was a bow and arrows, what could be in the other

44

package? It wasn't quite as long, but now it was equally intriguing. I turned my attention to it.

"Careful," said Pa.

Hmmm. This must be something really good if he's telling me to be careful. He didn't say that before I opened the other one, only after. I could not believe my eyes. As I opened the narrow end, I discovered a black, metal tube that looked like the barrel of a rifle, but it wasn't like any of the many toy rifles that I had in my cap gun collection. This was heavier and thicker. I quickly tore off the rest of the paper, which revealed that I was holding a .22 rifle! Again, the *real* thing! My heart leapt!

"Now listen closely," Pa began. "This is *my* rifle, but I bought it so you can use it. When you're old enough to own a gun, it'll be yours. In the meantime, it's kept under lock and key with my other guns. Get it?"

I got it! Wow! My own (sort of) real gun. Strangely enough, though, I had mixed feelings about this rifle. Sure, I was excited to get it, but it was very modernistic. The butt was fiberglass rather than wood. It didn't look like any of the rifles that the cowboys on TV used. So, in that sense, it was a little disappointing. But it *was* a *real* rifle! I loved my Dad.

Before supper that night, we finished opening the bow and arrow box, took out the six arrows and the paper targets. Pa had to string the bow - I wasn't strong enough. And I really didn't know how. He knew - because he read the instructions. There was a small leather finger guard that I managed to put on. I was ready. But, he had to shoot first.

The first paper target, bearing a picture of a deer, was taped to an old cardboard box, leaned up against an old aluminum folding chair and placed in an area of the yard that was backed by trees and bushes. At least if we didn't hit the target, we wouldn't be breaking any windows or impaling any neighbors.

The next Saturday morning, after breakfast, Pa announced that we were going to the shooting range to try out the new rifle.

"We're gonna meet Dave Brown there," he said.

We pulled into the parking lot just a few moments after Dave arrived. He bounded out of his car, opened the trunk and pulled out a knapsack. Slinging the knapsack over his shoulder, he walked up to my father's station wagon.

"Hi, Ed. Hi, Eddy!" He looked genuinely pleased to see me there. "Ready to try out the new rifle?"

I just nodded. Pa took a large wooden box out of the back and motioned to me.

"Your gun. You carry it."

I ran over and pulled the rifle out of the wagon and held it under my arm. We walked down to the range and put our gear on a wooden table. Pa opened the box, which held several pistols, some ammunition, ear phones and a telescope. He put his earphones around his neck and handed me a set of foam ear plugs.

"Better put these in now."

I was familiar with these from the times that he took me to the National Guard armory so that he could do some target shooting with his pistols. As soon as I put them in, I heard a whistle blow and a man announce on a loud speaker "Cease fire!" Only a few people had been shooting, and they were down the other end of the range.

Together, we walked out toward the back of the range and put up our paper targets. Dave had written our names on the targets with a think black crayon. DAVE. ED. ED, JR. When he put mine up, Dave turned to me, smiled and gave me a thumbs up. I smiled back.

Once we were gathered back at the table, Pa showed me how to load the rifle. He took a ramrod out of the stock, dropped in ten bullets, then re-inserted the rod and locked it. He showed me how to pull back the bolt and release the safety. Previously, I had been taught how to sight a gun, but Pa reviewed the steps with me. Soon, we heard the whistle again and we knew that it was safe to fire.

"Three rounds," commanded my father, as he pulled out the telescope.

Pop!

"High and to the right."

I took careful aim again, inhaled slowly, then squeezed the trigger.

Pop!

"Low and to the left."

Pop!

"Just in the black, about 6 o'clock."

He motioned to me to surrender the weapon as he gave the telescope to his friend. Pa shouldered the rifle, took aim.

Pop! Pop! Pop!

Dave peered through the scope, then took it away from his eye, shook his head, smiled and announced, "Two dead center in the bull's eye and one just outside at 4 o'clock!"

Pa was a good shot. No doubt about that. He had been shooting for many years. It was one of his passions. He gave a slight smile and toss of the head as he handed the rifle back to me.

"How many rounds do you have left?" he quizzed.

"Four," I replied.

"Go ahead."

I took aim and fired in rapid succession.

Pop! Pop! Pop! Pop!

Again, Dave looked through the scope.

"Not bad. Three in the black. One of them close to the bull's eye!"

"Load it up again," was the next command. "Five rounds this time, and take your time. Don't try to get fancy."

I shot again, taking more time. No one checked with the telescope. When I was done, Pa took the rifle again and emptied it into his target. We waited until Dave shot a few rounds with one of his own guns, then we heard the whistle again, "Cease fire!"

We walked out to check the targets. Where each bullet had punctured the paper, we placed a small piece of masking tape, so that we wouldn't have to keep changing the targets.

When the whistle blew again, I shot another ten rounds, and another. Meanwhile, my father started shooting his Colt .45 automatic and Dave was shooting a .22 six shooter. My ammunition was then exhausted. After another check and patching of the targets, I was out of ammunition, so I just sat back and watched the two men continue shooting.

Dave could see that I was bored just being a spectator, so he turned to Pa and said, "Why don't you let Eddy try the .45?"

"Are you kidding?" he answered. "There's too much of a recoil to it. It'd probably knock him on his ass and he'd shoot his foot off." He went back to shooting without even looking at me.

Dave made a face and motioned for me to come over to him. With a smile, he handed me the .22 pistol. "Give this a try. No kick to it."

I thanked him and then shot. He encouraged me to shoot all six bullets.

The next time my father started to load the clip for his pistol, Dave asked if he could take a closer look at the weapon. My father invited him to. Dave's eyes got that big look. He truly admired this gun.

"Want to try it?" asked Pa.

"Could I?"

"Sure, go ahead."

Dave shot off a few rounds at his target, then handed the gun back to its owner.

"That's really a nice gun," he said. "I've always wanted one of those. How much do you want for it?"

"You mean you want to buy it?" asked Pa. I could see that he was studying Dave's face.

"Yeah. How much?"

Pa looked thoughtfully, first at the gun, then at Dave, then at the gun again. Finally, he put the pistol back in Dave's hand.

"It's yours. Keep it."

This time, I thought Dave's eyes were going to pop out of his head.

"What? Are you serious, Sarge?" he blurted out. He stood there with his mouth open.

"Take it," my father said casually. "I have another .45 at home."

I knew and understood the look on Dave's face. It was probably the same look that I had when I opened up my rifle. Amazement, joy and unbelief! I never knew that my father could be so unselfish and generous. I admired that. *That was a really cool thing to do*, I thought.

Just around the block was the Drug Store. I probably went in there at least a dozen times every week. A quart of milk, a loaf of bread, the Sunday newspaper...just about everything, including that mysterious purchase that I was sometimes forced to make for my mother. She would give me a folded note.

"Give this to Alice and she'll know what to give you," Mom would say. She'd give me a few dollars. Alice was the woman who usually worked behind the counter. After I gave her the note, she would get a big paper bag and put a purple box into it, folding over the top of the bag. Without looking me in the eye, she would give me the change. Sometimes on the way home I would peek in the bag. But, I had no idea what "feminine napkins" were. Eventually, I asked my mother what they were and her response was an embarrassed, "Just something women use." We left it at that.

Comic books were my passion, especially super-hero comics. Of course, my favorite was the ever-popular *Superman*. What kid didn't wish he could fly and be invulnerable? To reinforce my devotion to the Man from Krypton, Kellogg's: The Greatest Name in Cereal sponsored the *Superman* TV show starring George Reeves. I was never stupid enough to really try to fly, like some kids did, but I wasn't beyond tying a towel around my neck and zooming around the house, sometimes jumping or diving from floor to sofa or bed. *The Flash* and *Batman* were also some of my favorites. These heroes were all the product of DC Comics. But, Doug introduced me to two intriguing characters that came out of the Harvey Publishing company: *The Fly* and *The Shield*. The Drug Store was the source of my supply for these springboards for my imagination.

One day, when I was perusing the latest issues of *Superman*, *Batman* and *The Flash*, debating as to which one I would spend my dime on, I looked up to see Frank the Druggist. He owned the Drug Store. He was also very tall and heavy set.

"I know what you've been doing," he stated quietly and calmly. I could feel my face turning red and getting hot. I wasn't absolutely sure at first what he was talking about, until he raised his eyebrows and stared at the comic book in my hand.

"I've been watching you for awhile now and I know that you've been stealing comic books from me."

Yes, I was afraid that was what he was going to say. I was in humongous trouble now.

"This is what I'm going to do. I'll make a deal with you. You go home now and get enough money to pay for every comic book you've stolen, bring it back to me, and I won't tell your parents about this. Okay, Eddy?"

"Okay," was my meek reply. I went home to search my room for money. Yes, I had been stealing comics for several months. I would mosey on back to the comic book rack, looking as nonchalant as possible. When I was sure that no one was looking, I would undo a few buttons on my shirt, fold the magazine in two vertically, and stuff it into the top of my pants. I'd button my shirt back up, and when I was certain that there was no tell-tale bulge, I would walk slowly out the door. Sometimes, I was even brazen enough to hide one comic in my shirt and actually go up to the counter to buy a second one, thus avoiding suspicion. Or so I thought, at least. Occasionally, on a Sunday, when I would go in to buy the Sunday newspaper, I would slip a comic into the paper before paying.

I truly had no idea how many purloined comics I had, but I was able to scrape together about a dollar and fifty cents. I went back to the Drug Store and presented Frank with the money.

"Now, don't do it again, or I'll be forced to tell your parents," he warned.

I agreed. I left being very embarrassed, but also quite impressed with Frank. He probably should have told my parents. After all, I was stealing, and it wasn't just once. It was multiple offenses. But, I guess he knew that I would be in a lot of trouble, and he knew that I was basically a good kid. He had watched me grow up, as he had all the kids in the neighborhood.

Chapter Eight

Emptying the trash and the garbage were more of those chores that I hated. It wasn't a simple process. Garbage was the easier of the two. After each meal, my mother would put all the left-over food scraps in a small pan on the kitchen counter. My sister and I would take turns emptying this. We would have to walk outside to the garbage pail, about twenty feet away from the house. This was a disgusting event, especially during the summer. First of all, it would stink! The garbage was picked up only once a week, so in the hot summer months it would be filled with white, fat, squirming maggots! When you emptied the pan of garbage into the pail, you had to bang it hard against the edge to make sure that all the food scraps fell in. This would succeed in causing a lot of the crawling bugs to fall back into the bottom of the pail. Gross!

Emptying the trash was more complicated. Under the kitchen sink was the waste basket, into which all of the non-food trash was put. The waste basket was then periodically emptied in two ways. At the bottom of the back steps lie the trash cans. These were used for glass, metal and other non-combustible waste. Once a week the trash cans were put at the end of the driveway and were emptied by the trash collectors. Combustible waste was taken to the incinerator way in the back yard and burned. At a fairly early age, I was given the task of emptying the trash and lighting the incinerator!

On one fateful day, I took the waste basket and a paper bag full of trash out from under the sink and walked it down to the trash barrels. This was another one of those chores that I hated, because it was often messy. Sometimes the cans or bottles were smeared with food from discarded napkins or paper towels. So, my hands would get all messy. Yuck! I quickly emptied the trash into the barrels and took the combustibles to the incinerator. As I dumped the waste basket into this large metal container, I caught a glimpse of something shiny and heard a tell-tale *clink* as some kind of can hit the bottom.

In itself this wasn't an uncommon occurrence. Later I would come back, after the fire had gone out and the incinerator cooled off, and sift through the ashes to pick out the can or bottle and throw it into the trash can. So, I didn't think much of it.

"Hey, Doug!" I shouted from my back yard. My friend stuck his head out of his bedroom window.

"Come on out!" I called. He gave a wave of consent and a few minutes later appeared at his back door. We walked up the street to the pig nut tree.

That day was a lazy day. We didn't feel ambitious at all. I brought several comic books with me, so we just sat under the tree and read.

"Hey, Doug," I finally said. "Did you ever dream that you could fly? I mean like Superman."

Raising his head up from the issue of *The Fly* that he was engrossed in, Doug said, "Yeah, I guess. Once or twice maybe."

"I have dreams like that all the time," I offered. "Had one last night. It was really weird, because all I had to do was start running, then I'd just bend my legs up and I'd keep going. Wish I could really do that."

"It'd sure save a lot of walking," Douglas added.

"Imagine being able to do that in school. Everybody would be so jealous," I said grinning.

"Like if you were playing baseball or basketball or something," said Doug.

We both were becoming very excited about the idea of "run flying." We were able to come up with many more examples of when it would be handy: crossing a street, going over puddles when it rains, or over broken glass on the ground.

The two of us were stretched out on the ground, staring up at the sky, just imagining and fantasizing about how great it would be to fly. Off in the distance we could hear the faints sounds of cars going by, birds chirping, and even a fire engine's siren.

"Too bad we can't really fly, ya know?" Doug remarked.

I began to feel the tug of reality myself.

"Yeah, too bad," I echoed.

We went back to our reading. The sun was very warm, but not too hot. Soon I felt a yawn well up in my throat. I opened my mouth wide and let it come out as I stretched my arms. A warm feeling of relaxation was beginning to take over my body and I felt myself drifting off.

Within moments, my body began to gently float up off the soft grass. I slowly rolled over and looked down. Several feet below, I could see the ground, and Douglas lying there. I realized that I had levitated about ten feet in the air. Cool! But, a shake of the head brought me crashing back to the ground where I woke up with a start.

I opened my eyes. Darn! It was only a dream. How long had I been asleep? As I turned to ask Doug this question, I saw that he was also asleep.

Sitting up, I looked over at my friend. Doug was snoring softly. I thought that was funny. Should I wake him up? Not yet. A small smile crept over my face as I watched him. I looked at my arm, then over at his. I looked back and forth several times. I had never really noticed it before, but my arms were hairier than Doug's. I guessed that made some sense...my hair was dark brown, his was light brown. But, then I leaned over and looked as close as I could at his face. His upper lip was bare. As I reached up to touch mine, I could feel the absence of fuzz because I was shaving.

Although Doug was at least a year older, and a foot taller, there were some ways that he didn't seem to be as mature as I was. My voice was getting deeper...his wasn't. He had a peculiar way of talking, too. It was hard to describe. Not exactly a lisp, more of a strange way that he held his mouth.

As I gazed at his sleeping body, I thought about how much I wished that he were my brother. I really wanted a brother...someone to talk to, to share secrets with. Sure, Doug and I did that, but there would be something different if we were in the same family. Now, I had to share him with his two brothers and his little sister. Oh, I had a sister, but that wasn't the same. Donna was older, and she was a girl. You can't talk to a girl the way you talk to another boy. Maybe if Doug had been my older brother I would have learned to swim or ride a bike. Oh, well. You don't have any control over who your family is. You get what you get and you make the best of it.

I was getting tired of sitting there, so I picked up a pig nut and threw it in the air above Douglas, so it would land on his stomach or his chest. Then I quickly laid back down and pretended to be asleep.

Douglas must have thought that the nut fell from the tree, because it was a few moments before he kicked my foot and called, "Hey, Schultz! Wake up!"

Finally, we packed up our comic books and walked back down the street. As we got closer to home, we saw two fire engines parked in front of my house. As soon as we spotted them, we began to run to see what was going on. The firefighters were rolling up their hoses. From where I stood I could see that a lot of the tall grass in the backyard was now in ashes. Where it had been a beautiful golden color hours before, now it was black and smokey.

My father was standing, hands on hips, talking to the Fire Chief. Pa turned in my direction. I knew I was in trouble.

"Get over here!"

Doug muttered an "Uh - oh!" under his breath as I walked forward. Pa's eyes were slightly squinted, and his left eyebrow was cocked. His face was red.

"You're responsible for this." He didn't yell. He spoke slowly and softly.

"What did I do?" My mind instantly flashed back to the moment that I emptied the waste basket into the incinerator and heard the *clink*.

"They found a can of hairspray in the incinerator," said my mother, who had been standing next to my father. "Apparently it exploded and set the back yard on fire."

Was I about to admit that I knew there was a can in the trash? No way.

"It must've been in the trash and I didn't know it. I wouldn't leave a hairspray can in there and set it on fire."

"I told you to always check and make sure there aren't any cans in the trash," was my father's gruff response. "From now on, no matches for you, kiddo. You just empty the trash, you don't light the incinerator."

"Awright," I cowered. "I'm sorry."

From that day on, I had a reputation in the neighborhood as a firebug. Any time there was a suspicious fire, I was the prime suspect. Not that this happened often, but there was a patch of tall grass across the street that occasionally did catch fire (I honestly don't know why or how) and I was usually blamed.

One night, at supper it was unusually quiet. Pa didn't say a single word, and had a very strange look on his face. I had never seen that look before. Whenever one of us would start to talk, Mom would hold her finger up to her lips. She didn't even tell us to be quiet, she only gestured.

When supper was over, Pa just walked to his bedroom and closed the door. This was very unusual. Most nights he either went into the den to watch TV or went down cellar to work on one of his projects or paint a sign. Sometimes he would do leatherwork. He had this big round slab of marble. He would make belts or wallets out of leather, then get his tools and stamp out really cool designs. He did mostly western-type decorations. But, that night, he just went to bed.

"What's wrong with Daddy?" Donna asked. I could see that she was quite worried.

"Yeah," I added. "Why's he so quiet?"

My mother picked up a few dishes and took them over to the sink. Her back was to us for a long while. Finally, she turned around, came back to the table and sat down. Her eyes were red, and tears were starting to build up.

"Your father's friend Dave..." she covered her mouth for a moment with her hand, then took a deep breath and continued, "Dave was...killed in a car accident this morning."

Although I had never been kicked in the stomach before, I knew then what it felt like. It was hard to breathe for a moment. A big knot was forming in my throat. Tears welled up in my eyes. I couldn't look at my mother or my sister. I just stared down at my empty plate. I never knew anyone who was dead before. I never really thought about people that I know being dead.

No one said anything after that. Donna and I washed and dried the dishes. I emptied the garbage and the trash. Then we all just went to bed. I didn't even think about television that night.

One day, my mother decided that I shouldn't just hang around during the summer. I should do something constructive. So, she talked my father into taking me to work with him. Big thrill.

Pa had his own business, a sign shop in the town square. He painted signs of all sizes and shapes, including big signs for businesses and small "sho-cards" for inside shops and shop windows. He was very good at this, and had an extremely steady hand and sharp eye. He also had a good sense of design. I thought it was great that my father had his own business.

"What's he going to do all day long?" was Pa's question.

"Well," she replied. "He can sweep up, clean the windows, empty the trash, maybe answer the phone, take Laddie for a walk."

Yes, our beagle Laddie went to work with Pa every day. He spent most of the time just sleeping in the window. Occasionally, he would jump up and bark at customers who walked by, or he just sat there and looked "cute."

"And you can pay him a little. Maybe fifty cents an hour."

Pa just "humphed" at that.

So, the next day I had to get up early and go to work with my father. Around seven o'clock I was aroused with, "Eddy, time to get up!"

I reluctantly threw on my clothes and slumped down the stairs. I could smell oatmeal cooking and coffee brewing. On the counter sat the familiar round, cardboard box with the guy in the funny black hat on the front and the word "Quaker" printed boldly beneath his picture. I loved the aroma of cooking oatmeal. I had a big bowlful, topped with sugar, cinnamon and milk. It warmed my innards and actually made me want to go back to bed.

"Come on, Butch, let's go," said Pa after we finished. He pointed to a paper lunch bag for me to take. I was also prepared with a book that I had snatched from the living room bookshelves, a book about World War II written by Ernie Pyle. Pa, Laddie and I all got into the station wagon and went off to work.

Eddy's Sign Shop was in the center of Braintree Square. There were two big glass display windows in front, one of which was Laddie's "stage" where he could show off for passers-by. The front room had a long easel-type workbench and one glass display case. The second room was a workshop where Pa kept all his supplies. The back room was a small office where he could keep his money, lunch, and other bookkeeping supplies.

My morning duties consisted of walking the dog, sweeping the floor, and emptying the trash into the dumpster out back. The morning went by fairly quickly. Several customers came in requesting small signs and posters. Pa took their orders and discussed the design with them. I just went about my chores. When it came time for lunch, I was sent to *Hennessey's*, a drug store on the corner, for coffee for Pa and a root beer for myself.

After lunch, I asked about my afternoon duties.

"I guess you can walk Laddie again, then just keep yourself amused. Read your book or something," was the response. So, I walked the dog again.

When I came back, Pa was working on a big sign that he had propped up on the front room work bench. I sat on a stool for awhile watching him. I was so amazed at how steadily he could hold a paint brush. He did all his lettering by hand. First, he would carefully sketch it out in pencil on a large sheet of white paper. When he had the lettering just right, he would score the paper with some kind of special tool that perforated the outline of the letters. Then he would tape the pattern onto the sign and rub the perforation with a charcoal pencil, leaving a light impression on the sign. After removing the paper he would set to work with his brushes. How I wished that my hands were as steady as his. How I wished that he'd offer to teach me how to do that.

I felt a lot of pride watching my father letter the sign. He was an artist in his own right. I was especially impressed when he would do gold leaf. This was a long and tedious process that included doing all the lettering in a special adhesive, then carefully placing thinner-than-paper gold leaf on the adhesive, allowing it to dry, then coating it with clear lacquer. Pa would never let me stand nearby when he did this. He told me that even the slightest breeze could ruin the project and waste gold.

The afternoon dragged. I read some of the book. It was an interesting, humorous account of regular soldiers. One amazing bit of trivia that I learned was about how to swat flies. Apparently, flies take off backwards, so when you want to swat a fly, you have to be sure to aim from behind him, instead of in front. At one point, I even went into the far back room, laid on the floor and took a nap.

About three o'clock Pa told me that he had to go out for awhile to deliver a sign. I was instructed to answer the phone, and if any customers came in to just tell them that he would be back in about an hour. I couldn't very well take a nap while my father was gone, so I took out a few pieces of plain white paper, taped them to the easel and tried my hand at designing some fliers for my magic shows. Using one of Pa's books, I copied my stage name in several different type styles. I didn't like the way they looked, so I threw several tries away. When Pa returned, I didn't see him approach the shop because I was engrossed in my designs.

"What are you doing?" he asked as he came in the door, ringing the little bell to announce the entrance of a customer.

"Oh!" He startled me. I crumpled up my last attempt and tossed it in the waste basket. "Nothing!"

Before we went home, I took Laddie for another walk.

I only went to work with Pa for a few days. We both finally decided that there wasn't enough work for me to do to make it worth while. He paid me ten dollars for my efforts, though.

As Doug and I sat in the log "boat" and continued our debate about the Flash and Johnny Jet, Doug's younger brother David jumped in to join us. The moment he landed, I noticed the patch on the sleeve of his jacket. The jacket seemed to be a little big for him.

"Hey, Dave, where did you get that Secret Squadron patch?" I inquired.

Before David had a chance to answer, Doug chimed in. "That's *my* old jacket. I just gave it to David last night. I got the patch on a jar of Ovaltine a couple of years ago."

"Son of a gun!" I said. "I almost had one of those. When they were giving them away, my Mom and I were shopping and I saw them. I really wanted one - real bad. I begged and begged, but she wouldn't get it. She said I wouldn't drink the Ovaltine 'cause I wouldn't like it. I promised that I'd drink it, but she didn't believe me! I think I probably cried my eyes out."

We all laughed at that.

Later, when the family was gathering for supper, I remembered the Secret Squadron patch.

"Hey, Mom," I said. "Remember a couple of years ago when I wanted you to buy that jar of Ovaltine so I could get a free Captain Midnight Secret Squadron patch, but you wouldn't get it for me?"

"I guess so," she replied as she put the mashed potatoes on the table.

"Well, Doug got one. I saw it today when his brother David was wearing one of Doug's old jackets. I didn't get one because you said I wouldn't like the Ovaltine!"

"That's right," Mom said. "It would've been a waste of money. I would have had to throw it away."

Pa raised his head. He had just become aware of our conversation.

"Ovaltine?" he said. "I love Ovaltine. I would've drank it."

Uh! I let out a huge sigh! If only my father had been with us when we were shopping. He would have been my hero! My savior! He would have helped me get a Captain Midnight Secret Squadron patch. Maybe   he   was   okay   after   all.

Chapter Nine

One morning I was awakened by my father's coughing. Only this time it didn't seem to stop. Mom came upstairs to wake us up.

"Donna, Eddy," she said somewhat frantically. "I'm taking your father to the hospital. He can't stop coughing and he's coughing up blood." Then, she and Pa rushed out to the car and were gone. My sister and I exchanged glances, but no words.

Late in the afternoon, Mom came home and explained that our father would be staying in the hospital for awhile. They would be doing tests to find out what was wrong. She explained that it was probably all related to his heavy smoking and the fact that he had worked at the ship yard some years ago and was exposed to asbestos.

This was very sobering. I wasn't sure how to feel. Pa had never been sick before, at least not as far as I could remember. So for him to be in the hospital meant that this must be very serious, especially since he didn't like doctors.

A few days later, Donna and I were allowed to visit Pa. We were told that we could only stay for a short time because he got tired quickly. I was stunned when I saw him. Sitting in the hospital bed, he looked so vulnerable. It seemed as though he had already lost a lot of weight. I felt a struggle inside. Part of me wanted to stay there to be with my father, but another part wanted to run out the door and head home for the logs or the pig nut tree.

"Hi, Butch," he said in a very weak voice.

"Hi," I said back. "How are you feelin?"

"I've been better. Kinda tired."

He looked tired, very tired. His skin was gray. His eyes were drooping. His shoulders were slumped. His hands and arms were down by his sides, like dead weights. He didn't move at all. There was food on the tray next to his bed, but it had not been touched. I was scared. I wondered if he was going to get well.

"The doctors say that your father has to stay a few more days," Mom said, her voice trembling. She had taken several days off work in order to go to the hospital to stay with Pa. She was tired, too. Usually Mom was very energetic, but now she was quiet and just sat.

Although it seemed as though we were there for hours, it was only about twenty minutes before we had to leave. Most of the time had been spent in silence. Just sitting there looking at each other.

In the next few days, my father's health did not improve. Soon he wasn't able to speak and had to write notes in order to be understood. And even then, he was so weak that his handwriting was often illegible and he had to try several times, becoming more frustrated with each attempt. His appetite was gone. Eventually they had to feed him with a tube, which he pulled out several times. I'm sure he didn't like being so helpless.

About two weeks after Pa went into the hospital we were visiting him again. This time he was out in the hallway in a wheel chair. He looked so tired. At this point he was having trouble focusing on what was going on around him. He never looked at me or seemed to know that I was there. He just sat and stared. Was this the last time that I would see him alive? The thought pulled and tugged at my head. I didn't want to think this way.

It was time to leave and Mom and Donna stood up to go.

"I want to stay for a minute," I said. "You two go ahead. I'll be right there."

They left. I missed my father. I missed his gruff voice. A tear formed in my eye and a lump in my throat. Standing close, I reached out my right hand and gently caressed his head. All I could do was to whisper to him.

"Happy trails, Pa. I love you."

I reached over and softly kissed his head. This was something that a parent would do to a child...it shouldn't be a child doing it to his parent, I thought. With tears streaming down my cheeks, I turned and left.

The next afternoon I couldn't bring myself to go to the hospital with my mother and sister. I was weak myself. No energy. Just a feeling of sadness. So, I stayed home and sat in front of the television. The time dragged. I don't remember what I watched, or even just what day it was.

Suppertime came and I was still alone. There hadn't been any word from my mother. I made myself a sandwich and went back to the den to watch TV. The telephone rang. It startled me! I spit out the food in my mouth and ran to the phone. I answered it.

"Hello."

"Hello, Eddy," my mother said. Her voice sounded very strange. "We're still at the hospital. Your father has taken a turn for the

60

worse." I could hear the tears in her voice. Then there was a shuffling sound. In the background I could hear her saying to my father, "Say 'hi' to Eddy."

What an odd thing for her to say. She told him to say hello to me as he lay dying. I guess she was so overcome that she wasn't thinking about what she was saying.

"I'm going to put the phone to his ear so your father can hear you," she said to me.

More shuffling and rustling sounds.

"I love you, Dad. I always have and I always will."

That was all I could say. I hadn't called my father 'Dad' in quite some time. It just slipped out.

"We have to hang up now. We'll be home soon. Go to bed."

I hung up, went to bed and cried until I fell asleep.

The next morning, when I woke up, I knew that my father was gone. No one woke me up. I went downstairs for breakfast and my mother was sitting at the kitchen table, tears in her eyes. When she saw me come into the room, she shook her head as she looked at me. She was biting her lip and couldn't speak. I stood there for a long moment, staring into space. My stomach felt very empty, but not because I was hungry.

I didn't call for Doug as I usually did. I just walked up the street and over to the pig nut tree. The sky was slightly overcast, although it was warm. Birds chirped and crickets creaked, but I didn't notice. There was the pig nut tree, straight and strong as ever, so I walked over to it and leaned my back against the sturdy trunk.

The view was the same as always, but it seemed a little different that day. Maybe because the sun wasn't shining. I don't know. The world seemed smaller somehow. Emptier maybe. Not as exciting. Many times when I would stand beneath this tree, my imagination would soar. I would see myself as many of my favorite TV and movie heroes, and have imaginary adventures. But not that day. My brain seemed to be in neutral...just coasting.

I didn't even hear the grass crinkle when he approached. I became aware of Doug's presence when he put his hand on my left shoulder. Neither of us exchanged words of greeting...they didn't seem to be necessary or even appropriate. Doug just nodded his head, and I nodded mine. We stood there staring out at the sky. Every now and then my eyes would fill with tears. I'd wipe them away with my hand.

A few times, I tried to remember some of the things that Pa and

I used to do together, but for some reason it just wouldn't happen. It was all a blur and a buzz. No happy memories. Nothing. Just a deep feeling of emptiness, almost like there was nothing inside my body. No heart, no stomach, no lungs. Just an empty shell.

Finally, I slid my back down the tree and sat on the ground. Doug sat, too. His hand was still on my shoulder. My head drooped between my knees and I began to sob. Now my insides felt as though they were filled with tears, tears that wanted to come out, to wash something away. As I started to cry, I could feel Doug's hand and arm move, until he had circled my shoulders.

At the same time, I felt very alone and not alone. My father was gone. I would never see him or talk to him again. Despite the fact that we did not always get along and that he constantly criticized me, I loved him. I hadn't really known him, and now I would never have the chance to know him. But, my best friend was there. He was with me during a very difficult and confusing time. His arm around my shoulder suddenly reminded me of the night that I thought of Abraham Lincoln being dead.

It was then that I realized why I was grieving most. It wasn't just because I missed my father, it was more because I missed what I never had with my father...and what I never *would* have with him.

Then, I could feel Doug's arm pull me in to him. His other arm went around my shoulders and his head bowed down to touch mine. On my scalp I could feel the heat of his head. He began to sob. It was like he was feeling my pain, my grief. Maybe he was even grieving something of his own. I didn't know. I only knew that my pain was beginning to subside a little. It felt as though we were brothers, sharing the same pain.

A warmth began to spread throughout my body. As I opened my tearful eyes, I realized that the sun was shining now. We both put our heads up at the same time. We looked at one another and smiled. Words still were not necessary. We stayed a while longer, tossing pig nuts and pebbles into the tall grass. Then we went home in silence.

The next morning, there was a knock at the back door. It was Doug. That was strange. He never did that before. Usually we'd just stand out in the yard and yell to each other.

"Hi, Doug," I said through the screen door. "What's up?"

"Hi, Edd. My Dad gave me some money and said I should take you to see a movie. *The Time Machine* is playing at the Strand. Wanna go?"

Time Machine? That sounded intriguing. Right up my alley.

"Sure. Let me just check with my mother."

Maybe this was a good idea. Maybe this would take my mind off my grief. I darted inside and found my mother straightening cushions in the living room. She had decided to take some more time off from work. She easily agreed to my request.

Doug and I took the bus to Quincy and hung around the stores for awhile waiting for the first showing to begin. When we entered, Doug bought popcorn and Coke for each of us. We settled into our seats.

What a movie! It was turn of the century England. Rod Taylor played an inventor named George who was obsessed with time. He described it as the fourth dimension and told his friends that he was making a machine that would allow him to travel back and forth in time. They thought he was crazy. Only one of his friends, Philby, was supportive at all. I instantly identified with "George." Although he had friends, he was almost alone in his own world of creativity and invention. He had a passion for time travel that no one shared. I even thought his clothes were cool! He wore a plaid smoking jacket and a gray vest.

As the story progressed, George traveled into the future, where he met two different races of people: the peaceful Eloi, who lived above ground, and the evil Morlocks, who lived in caves under the ground and captured Eloi people so that they could eat them! Really cool. And he fell in love with this really beautiful girl. Even that was okay. I was beginning to appreciate girls myself.

When the movie was over, we talked about it all the way home on the bus. Where and when would we go if we had a time machine? Doug wanted to go to the future. I wanted to go to the past. I wanted to see the Revolutionary War, meet Abraham Lincoln, go to the Battle of New Orleans, maybe even become a pirate like Jean Lafitte. I could zap through time and have lots of adventures. It wasn't until that night, as I lay in bed that I thought about going back in time to see my father, maybe even to meet him when he was my age.

Maybe, just *maybe*, I could build my own time machine. I had to get more information about time travel. That would mean a trip to the library. I would start by reading the original H.G. Wells novel, then see what other non-fiction books I could find about time travel. Much to my disappointment, the only material I could find on time travel was either

63

science fiction or excerpts in a physics textbook that were way beyond my comprehension. So much for that idea.

I could hear my mother shuffling around in her bedroom, so I peeked inside. She was going through my father's bureau, looking at his clothes, handkerchiefs, jewelry, etc.

"Come on in," she said. Her eyes were red and there were still tears streaking down her cheeks. "I was just going through your father's things. Maybe there are some things you'd like to have or you could use."

I walked in and sat on the bed without saying a word.

"You may as well take his handkerchiefs. You can use them. He has some cufflinks here. Take them." She continued to look through the drawers. Toward the back of the top drawer was a cigar box. Mom placed it on the bed. She opened it to reveal a collection of various objects, some related to his prior military career - Army insignia for shirts, hats. Some medals for marksmanship.

"Would you like these?"

"Sure," I said quietly. Then, we both noticed two folded pieces of paper. The first was a piece of newspaper a few inches square. Mom opened it up and looked at it. I could see that it was from the classified section. She smiled gently and looked up at me.

"I think you might like to have this," she said as she handed it to me.

In the center of the paper was a red oval outlining a small advertisement that read: *Harry Voldini, the Teenage Conjuror will present magic shows for children's parties. Call VI 3-5783.* I looked up at my mother.

"Why did he have this?" I asked.

"He was very proud of you for doing that, for being so enterprising," was her answer.

"But, he never said anything," I responded.

"No," she said. "He didn't say anything to *you*, but he did tell *me*. That was just his way. He wasn't sure what to say to you." As she spoke, she opened up the second paper. It was a piece of white paper, crinkled quite a bit. As soon as she saw what it was, she handed it to me as well. It was one of my discarded sketches from the sign shop. It had *The Amazing Voldini* written on it several times, using different type styles. It was one of the papers that I had thrown in the trash. Apparently, my father had retrieved it later. I could feel a tear forming

64

in my right eye.

"He really was very proud of you," Mom repeated.

"But, why didn't he like me?" I asked as the tears began to roll down my cheeks.

"What makes you think he didn't like you?" Mom asked.

"He never told me he loved me or even liked me. He always made fun of me. He seemed like he was always disappointed in me," I sobbed.

"Well," Mom began. "Your father never really knew how to be a father. You see his grandfather died very young, so *your* grandfather, Dad's father, never had a father as he was growing up, so he didn't learn how to be a father to *his* son, *your* father. And they all came from a different generation, a time when men didn't express their feelings. So, Dad didn't *know* how to tell you that he loved you. He didn't *know* how to express his feelings for you."

I guess I understood what she was saying, but it just didn't seem fair. I would have liked to hear my father tell me that he was proud of me or that he loved me. Hearing it was very important.

"When you were born, your father swore that he was going to be a good father to you; that he wasn't going to let happen to you what happened to him. I guess it was just more than he could handle, because he never knew what to do. He wanted you to be a real man. He wanted you to be tough. Whenever he saw you doing something that he thought wasn't real 'manly', I guess he just wasn't sure how to handle it. Do you understand?"

"Yeah, I guess so."

Mom turned and looked at Pa's gun cabinet, next to the bed.

"By the way, when you're old enough, you'll get all his guns. That's what he wanted."

I looked at the gun cabinet, too. Part of me was excited about inheriting the collection, but another part was disappointed that I never truly had a chance to share them with my father. I would rather have had my father back than have the gun collection.

"After your father's funeral we need to go shopping for clothes for school," Mom added. "Now, why don't you take those things up to your room. If I find anything else that you might like, I'll set it aside for you."

I took my mementos up to my room and put them in my special drawer, my "treasure" drawer.

Chapter Ten

I had never been to a funeral or a wake before. When my mother, sister and I walked into the funeral home to get ready for the wake, it was very strange. The funeral director, a tall, thin man, brought us back to the room where Pa was laid out in a casket. Pa looked weird. His face had all kinds of makeup on it and his mouth was very unnatural looking. My mother and sister both cried for a long time, but I just stood there staring at him. I couldn't believe that he was really dead. I'd never hear his voice again, never smell his stale tobacco smell or hear him cough. Never again would I smell boot polish or his special fried eggs with bacon. It just didn't seem fair. I wanted to shake him and wake him up. I wondered why this was called a wake. Maybe it had something to do with waking up dead people. But, they wouldn't wake up because they were dead. I didn't get it.

Then people started to arrive. We were supposed to stand near the casket and greet people. I was told to thank them for coming. But, I really didn't want to talk to anybody. I didn't even want to stand there. So many of these other people were crying, especially the women. The big criers were on my mother's side. Her parents came to America from Sicily when they were young, so everyone on Mom's side of the family was Italian, and Italians show their emotions very openly. My aunts all cried and cried. They would come over to me, look at me and say, "Oh, Little Eddy...." then start crying into their handkerchiefs. I didn't know what to say to them, so I just smiled awkwardly. My aunts on Pa's side of the family were more reserved. They cried, but weren't quite as dramatic.

Although I wasn't really listening, I did overhear bits and pieces of conversation.

"He was such a wonderful man."

"He was so young. I guess it was just his time."

"When your number's up...you have to go."

"I'm sure he's in a better place."

"He was a very good man."

"God must have had other plans for him."

Early in the evening, Douglas and his parents came. They didn't stay for long. Doug and I went out back and hung out in the parking lot for awhile. There wasn't much conversation.

"We can't go to the funeral tomorrow," explained Doug. "Cuz we're Catholics, ya know, so we're not supposed to go into a Protestant Church or we'll go to hell or something."

That was okay. Although it would have been good to have my best friend nearby, I understood. I didn't want Doug to go to hell because of me.

When we got home that night, I watched a little TV. I was hungry so I had a snack. A cup of Hershey's Cocoa and some Saltine crackers with jelly. The jelly was homemade by my father's Aunt Bertha. Aunt Bertha was an older woman who spent most of her life as a single woman. I liked her a lot. She sometimes used to babysit for us when I was younger. She always listened and seemed to pay attention when I spoke, even if it was just to tell a crumby kid joke. She even showed me a few magic tricks. When I pried the thick wax seal off the jelly there was a little bit of mold. My mother told me to just scoop it out and everything would be okay, so I did. I had lots of crackers and jelly, because the jelly was delicious.

The funeral was in the morning. A limousine picked us up and took us to the church. We went to an Episcopal Church in Quincy. It was a very old, stone building. We walked down the aisle behind the casket and sat in the front row. The minister was Mr. Porteus, an older, somewhat heavy man with a strange right eye. My mother said he had a "cast" in his eye. I don't remember what he said, but I always loved to hear him talk. He had a very deep, melodious voice and a special way that he phrased many things.

At one point in the service we all had to stand. My mother was on one side of me and my Aunt Mary was on the other. Suddenly, I felt very weak. The room started to spin as my hearing began to fade out. My knees became soft, and I went down! Auntie Mary must have seen what was happening, because she guided me down onto the pew, so I didn't actually fall. The service went on, as I sat there in a fog. I was limp and had no strength. I wasn't sick to my stomach, but I felt as though I had no body, just a head. After what seemed like a long time but was probably only a few minutes, my head cleared and I regained some of my strength...just enough to be guided out of the pew and into the procession as we left the church.

When we got into the limo again, my mother asked, "What happened?"

"I don't know," I said. "Maybe I got sick on Aunt Bertha's jelly. It had mold, you know."

"Don't be silly," my mother replied. "I'm sure it wasn't the jelly...and don't you dare say anything to Aunt Bertha. You don't want to hurt her feelings."

I wouldn't hurt Aunt Bertha for the world. She was my favorite aunt...well, great-aunt.

By the time we arrived at the cemetery I had gained back most of my strength. I took a few deep breaths and felt a lot better.

Mr. Porteus was about to begin when my mother walked over to him and said something softly. I couldn't hear what it was. But, then he spoke.

"We'll begin in a few moments. Some family members have not yet arrived."

I looked around to see who was missing, but I wasn't sure. A few minutes later an old car pulled up. The location of the grave was on top of a small but steep hill, which we all had to walk up. When I looked down and saw who we were waiting for I groaned silently. It was Aunt Bertha and Uncle Lester. They had recently been married...and they were in their seventies! Aunt Bertha was the first to get out. She had been driving. Uncle Lester had been having trouble with his knees, so he walked with two canes. My great-aunt opened the door for him and helped him out of the car. Poor old guy. He was very frail. I liked Uncle Lester. He was always friendly and always asked what I was doing in school, or just for fun. He would listen when I told him about my hobbies and interests.

Aunt Bertha handed Uncle Lester his canes as he emerged from the car. They made a cute couple. Once he was on his feet he started talking to Aunt Bertha. She walked to the back door, opened it and reached inside. She pulled out...a roll of toilet paper.

From atop the little hill we could all see this, and I noticed that a few of the grown-ups started to smile. I thought it was pretty funny. Toilet paper! What was that for? Then I understood. Uncle Lester's shoulders began to shake and we could hear him sobbing. He really liked my father, so I'm sure the loss was hard on him. Aunt Bertha took about a foot of paper off the roll and handed it to him. He sobbed and blew his nose into the tissue.

My Auntie Kitty was stifling a laugh. My mother just looked away. Donna held her hand over her mouth.

Uncle Lester regained his composure and with his companion at his side, he began to walk up the hill. After about ten feet he stopped, then started to cry again. He let out a wail. Aunt Bertha unrolled more paper and handed it to him. Sniff, sniff. Honk!

It was really strange that something so funny was happening during such a serious time. More and more of the adults were smiling. Some were putting their hands over their mouths, others turned away. Even the funeral director turned his back so he wouldn't see what was going on. I looked at our minister and he was smiling too, but he was also shaking his head gently.

Again the old couple resumed their journey up the hill. This time they made it about fifteen feet, when Uncle Lester broke down again. More toilet paper. More crying. I almost lost it this time. My stomach was aching because I was holding in the laughter.

Finally, they made it! Poor Uncle Lester.

We listened to Mr. Porteus say a few more words, and then it was over. What a shame. It had taken the old couple about ten minutes to walk up, and the graveside service was only another ten minutes.

We went back home. Everybody came back to the house. There was all kinds of food...mostly Italian. I always looked forward to my grandmother's meatballs. She made these great meatballs that had no meat, only breadcrumbs and eggs. And her spaghetti sauce was out of this world! No one could make it like Grandma.

It was warm enough so we set up some tables outside in the back yard. Everybody brought lawn chairs. It was almost like a holiday...like fourth of July or Labor Day when the whole family would go on a picnic, except this was at my house. It was strange. All these people, eating all this food, and my father was gone. I heard people telling stories about when my father was younger. Some people were joking, some people were drinking beer.

Uncle Charlie, my favorite uncle, was my father's younger brother. They looked a lot alike, except Pa had dark brown hair and Uncle Charlie had blond hair. He came over to me and ruffled my hair. He looked at me for a long time, then said, "You know, your father was very proud of you. I know he probably never said it to you. He wasn't much of a talker. But, he did tell me that. I thought you should know."

I politely thanked him. It was nice to know that, but it was a shame that I had to hear it from my uncle at my father's funeral, instead of from my father himself.

That night, after everyone was gone and the cleaning up was finished, my mother sat down heavily on the sofa, in the same spot where Pa always used to sit. She breathed a deep sigh. Even though she was always made up perfectly, there were dark circles around her eyes. As I walked past her, on my way up stairs, she beckoned to me.

"Eddy, come and sit down."

I stopped walking and sat next to her.

"Are you okay?" she asked. "Do you want to talk about this?"

I just shook my head and sat there quietly for a few moments. Then I had an idea. I did want to talk about my father, and the funeral, but I didn't want to talk to my mother. We had always been able to talk before, but this was different.

"I think I want to talk to Father Pierce."

Father Pierce was one of the ministers at our church. He must have been about forty years old and had two children - a son my age and a daughter a few years older than my sister. He was a nice guy, and I felt that I would be able to talk freely with him.

"Do you want me to call him for you and see if you can go to see him tomorrow?"

"Okay," I sighed. I was very tired, and even though there were a lot of question swirling around in my head, I just wanted to go to bed.

Episcopalians are sort of Protestant, sort of Catholic. Maybe a combination of both. Our church had two ministers. Mister Porteus was the Rector. He was the boss. The Curate was Father Pierce. He was the second in command. I was never quite sure why one was called "Mister" and the other was called "Father." But, I liked calling Father Pierce "Father." Somehow it felt both holy and warm at the same time. It helped me feel a closeness to him. And at that point, I needed a father.

We pulled into the parking lot of this historic Gothic-style church, walked up the old stone steps and through the two massive red doors. The door to the office was already open, so I knocked on the door and walked in. Father Pierce looked up from the heavy oak desk, took off his glasses and began to stand up. He wore a black short-sleeved shirt with a white clerical collar. Around his neck was a silver chain that held a black wooden cross. I was always fascinated by this collar because it was hard to figure out how it stayed on. Because Father Pierce wasn't wearing a jacket, the back of the collar was visible. There was some kind of brass button or stud that stuck out of the back. It was easy to understand that this held it to the back, but what about the

71

front?

"Come on in, Eddy," he said in a calm, low voice. I cringed a little when he called me that. It made me feel like a little kid. But, I guessed that was okay then.

"Thank you, Father," I replied as I entered. He motioned to the chair next to the desk.

"Have a seat. I'm really sorry about your father. Am I correct in assuming that's why you wanted to see me?" We both sat down.

"Yes, it is," I said. "I have some questions."

"That's fine. I'll do the best I can to answer them."

There were so many questions that I wasn't sure where to start at first. I sat for a moment trying to sort this out and also trying to talk. Thinking about my father suddenly caused my throat to tighten. I could feel tears starting to form. My fists clenched and my right hand went up to my mouth. Father Pierce gently pushed a box of tissues in my direction and quietly spoke.

"Take your time. I know it's not easy to talk about this."

We sat in silence for a few minutes. Finally, I took a deep breath, exhaled and was ready to speak.

"People have been saying a lot of things that confuse me. I'm not sure what to believe."

"Okay."

"For instance, someone said that God needed my father more than we did, so He took him."

Father Pierce gently nodded, but then took a little breath and shook his head back and forth.

"In the midst of grief, people often say things that they think will bring comfort to others. They're well-meaning, but based on mistaken assumptions."

I was pretty sure that I followed what he was saying. But, I needed some reassurance, so I asked, "Did God really take my father?"

Father's head shook again.

"God doesn't *take* people. I don't believe that our faith tells us that He chooses or determines when people are going to die. But, when they do, He *receives* them into His arms."

That was a relief to hear. I was ready to become an atheist. I knew that an atheist is a person who doesn't believe in God. I didn't want to believe in a God who would take my father away from me.

"Good," I said. "I don't think it would be fair if He took people just because He wanted them."

"That's right. Think of it this way. God is our Father in heaven. He's our Divine parent. If you were a parent, and you had the power of life and death over your children, would you take their lives just because you were lonely?"

"No. Of course not," I replied.

"Neither would God. So, God didn't take your father because he was lonely or because he needed another angel. Your father died of sickness. And when he died, God received him and welcomed him into His arms."

That made sense to me and I felt much better about God.

"God is a God of love," Father Pierce continued. "He wants what is best for us. But, He's also a God who gives us free will. He doesn't manipulate our lives. He allows them to unfold, and He is always with us to give us the strength we need to live them."

"So does that mean that when people say, 'it's your time' or 'when your number's up' it's not that God has decided it's time for you to die?" I asked.

"That's right, Edd. Although in His omniscience, He knows *when* you will die, he doesn't determine it beforehand."

Omniscience. That was quite a word. I wasn't sure what that meant.

"What does 'omni....'"

"'Omniscience' means God's ability to know all. God knows all that's going to happen, but He doesn't cause it all to happen."

"Wow!" I said. "I'm not sure I understand *that*, but that's okay."

I liked talking with Father Pierce. He didn't talk down to me with cute little stories. He spoke to me like I was an adult. He sort of reminded me of the two librarians who got books for me at the main library.

A few days later, my mother and I went shopping for school clothes. This was usually something that I dreaded - being dragged around from store to store looking for pants, shirts, shoes. But, this time I was looking forward to shopping for some new clothes. I would be entering junior high in a few weeks. No longer would I be a kid going to elementary school. I would now be an almost-teenager, a step closer to being an adult. I wanted to be an adult. I wanted to grow up. And I wanted some grown up clothes.

The Time Machine had quite an effect on me. Although I had given up the idea of time travel, I was still quite taken with the character. I wanted to be like him. I even wanted to dress like him. I felt that this would make me look more grown up. In the movie, Rod Taylor, as the time traveler, wore dark blue pants, white shirt, gray vest, dark tie and a smoking jacket that was blue plaid with red lapels. Obviously I wasn't going to wear a smoking jacket to school, but maybe we could find something close.

Of course, I didn't tell my mother that I wanted to look like the time traveler, but I did tell her that I had some definite ideas about what I wanted. The compromise included blue pants, an olive drab vest, a dark blue necktie, and a cranberry sports coat. Cranberry was the "in" color that year, so that was okay. When I said that I wanted a vest, my mother objected.

"You'll look like an old man," she protested.

"But, I want a vest, Ma. I think it'll be cool!"

We did get the vest. I didn't exactly look like Rod Taylor, but when I put on my outfit, I felt older, more adult. Of course, the color combination probably gave any onlookers a headache, but I was happy.

I managed to convince my mother that I also *needed* to have a new magic trick. Probably because she was feeling sorry for me, she agreed to stop by the Joke Shop on our way home. She didn't come in with me, partly because it wasn't easy to find a parking space when leaving Quincy Square, and partly because she didn't like to see the fake dog pooh, fake vomit, and whoopy cushions that were on sale.

Pete showed me his latest acquisition, a pocketknife that changed color. He showed me both sides, which were white, then he gave it a shake and both sides of the handle changed to black. He did this several times, back and forth. I was suitably impressed. I presented the ten dollar bill that my mother had given me, and after I received my change, Pete took me behind the counter to reveal the secret. I took the knife home and practiced all night.

Over the course of the next two weeks, I began to get used to my father not being around. It was very strange. Watching television was a new experience. No longer did I lay on the floor with my head on the hassock. I sat on the couch and put my feet on the hassock. I got to choose whatever programs I wanted to see, except when Donna really wanted to see something. Instead of asking Pa if I could have a snack during commercials, I just got up and helped myself. Westerns were still my favorite. I began to see more and more actors who resembled my father in one way or another. One show that we used to watch together was *Sea Hunt* with Lloyd Bridges as Mike Nelson, the scuba diver. Bridges had my father's eyes and eyebrows. George Nader in *The Man and the Challenge* had Pa's haircut. But, nobody had his voice.

One day, I stood on the back porch and looked out at the yard. This was *my* yard now. *I* had to take care of it. Mowing the lawn was no longer an option. I had to do it and I had to do it well. No more complaints. I looked at the apple trees. We had two of them, both Macintosh. I would have to pick the apples and clean up the ones that dropped. When fall came I would have to rake the leaves and burn them on the curbside. When it was winter I would have to shovel the snow. No more excuses. My mother and sister certainly wouldn't do these things.

I went down to the cellar and looked through the area that Pa used as a workshop. He had all kinds of tools. These were mine now. If I didn't already know what they were or how to use them, I'd have to learn. Picking up a hammer and a screwdriver, I held them tightly and thought about the things that he had made for me over the years. Swords, boxes, forts. I wondered how many toys he had put together for me at Christmas. When I browsed through his brushes and paints, I regretted that he hadn't taught me more. I knew that I would never be able to paint a sign like he did. My hands just weren't as steady as his, nor my eyes as sharp. I wondered what would become of the sign shop. There was nothing I could do about that, not at age twelve anyway.

Then I spotted it in the corner of the cellar near the door to the shed. The lawnmower. For so long it had been my arch nemesis. I had hated that machine. There was an odor of damp grass and gasoline. It stung my nose and caused a slightly nauseous feeling in my throat. But, now we had to be friends. Now it was *my* lawn mower. Not just *the* lawn mower, but *my* lawn mower. My hands reached out and took hold of the grips.

All right, boy, I thought, *it's up to us now. We have a job to do.*

At night sometimes, I would lie on my bed and look around my room. There was the attache case that Pa had lettered for me. On the bureau was the cowboy hat that I had cherished so much. On the other end of the bureau was the short-wave radio receiver that we had built together one Christmas. Well, actually, he built it and I watched. Once in a while he would let me assemble a part. Memories of all the good things seemed to pop right up into my mind. I wasn't angry with him any more. Although I still thought of him as "Pa" the word took on a new meaning for me. It was something special. Every kid called their father "Dad" or "Daddy" but my father was "Pa." There seemed to be a sense of strength to the word itself.

One morning I woke up early and went down to the kitchen. I took out the small sauce pan, the round cardboard box of oatmeal, and for the first time I read the package to see what you needed to do to cook it properly. My mother came into the kitchen.

"What are you doing?" she asked.

"Making oatmeal. You want some?"

She hesitated for just a moment. "Sure, I'll take some. Do you need any help?"

"No, that's okay. I need to learn how to do this eventually anyway. Might as well be now," I said.

Chapter Eleven

I was ready to fool my friend. For hours I had practiced the secret moves for my color-changing pocketknife. I was ready. When we arrived at the pig nut tree, I nonchalantly took the knife out of my pocket, opened it and began to carve my initials in the bark of the tree. It took a few minutes before Doug noticed, because he was hungry and was cracking nuts.

"Hey!" he said. "Is that a new jackknife?"

"This?" I asked, trying to be blase. "Oh, yeah, I guess it is."

"When'd you get it?"

"Oh, when my mother took me shopping for school clothes."

At that point, he could only see the white side.

"Why'd you get a white one?"

That was my opportunity. I had my story ready for him. As I spoke, I turned the knife over and over in my hand, making the secret move, so that it appeared to be white on both sides.

"Well, I was looking at two knives. There was this one, which is white...."

Then, I did another secret move to change it to black, and kept showing it on both sides.

"...and there was another one that was black. I kinda liked the black one, and at first I couldn't decide...white...or black...white...or black...."

Each time I mentioned a color, I would make the secret move and change it to that color, then to the other. Doug just stood watching me, his mouth open.

"Finally, I decided on the white one!" As I said these words, I changed it to white, showed it quickly, then put it in my pocket.

"Hey, wait a minute!" shouted Doug as he approached me. "Let me see that! How did you do that? Come on, *Voldini*! Show it to me!"

Again, I was ready. I switched the knife for the one that was only white, pulled it back out and tossed it to my friend. "Here you go!"

He caught the knife, then quickly turned it over and over several times. He tried to pull the handle apart, tried to slide it back and forth, but to no avail.

"How did you do that?" Doug was getting frustrated. "Do it again." He gave me the knife back. I wasn't expecting that. How could I switch it again? I pushed it in my pocket.

"What? I didn't do anything. I just showed you my knife." I played dumb.

"Do it again," he demanded. "Make it change color!"

"Okay," I reluctantly agreed. Reaching into my pocket I pulled out the special knife. "I got the white one." I showed both sides. "But, I coulda got the black one." I changed the color and showed both sides again.

"How did you do that?"

"Very well, I thought," I said with a haughty nod of my head.

"Very funny," Doug countered. "Tell me how you did that!"

"Magic!"

He was getting frustrated. He lowered his voice.

"How did you do it?"

I looked back and forth, as though checking to see if anyone was listening or watching. Then I leaned in close and whispered, "Can you keep a secret?"

"Yeah," he answered softly, his eyes getting larger in expectation.

I quickly lifted my head and spoke in a normal but somewhat sarcastic voice.

"So can I!"

Suddenly, Doug lunged forward and tried to grab the knife. I was quick enough to avoid him and shove it back deep into my pocket. Then, he charged at me. I turned to run, but wasn't quick enough. My body went crashing to the ground, face first. My glasses flew off my face and landed a few feet away. Doug recovered, stood over me, grabbed me by the waist and flipped me over. I was on my back in an instant.

Before I knew what happened, Doug was on top of me. My shoulders were pinned down by his knees. His butt was on my mid-section and his feet were holding down my legs. I tried to flip my legs up and hit him in the back, but his feet were too strong. I could hardly breathe because of the pressure on my body. I could feel the circulation being cut off in my arms.

"Now," Doug said as he folded his arms across his chest. "Give me the knife and show me how it works."

"But, it's supposed to be a secret, Doug," I pleaded.

"Okay, but I'm supposed to be your *best* friend and I promise I won't tell anyone. You can trust me."

A flood of thoughts rushed through my brain. Douglas *was* my best friend. He was always there for me. He never lied to me. He always treated me with respect. He never made fun of me. Then, I saw a flash of my father's friend Dave. Then my father was standing in the water, saying to me, "You can trust me." I felt scared. No, I couldn't trust him. Doug was looming over me saying, "Trust me." I *could* trust *him*.

Being a magician was becoming more and more important to me. I wanted to do it right. One of the cardinal rules of magic is: do not reveal the secret. I wanted to be true to this code of ethics. But, my best friend had me in a position where I almost *had* to tell him.

I saw Doug reach his arm behind his back. I could feel his hand going into my pocket. There was nothing I could do. He would easily be able to get the knife. But, somehow, I also knew that if I genuinely told him to stop, he would.

I let out a breath of submission.

"Okay," I sighed. "I'll tell you tomorrow."

He crossed his arms in front of his chest again and stared at me. "Tomorrow?!? Why tomorrow? Why not now?"

This situation was a real dilemma. I really didn't want to have to tell him. Maybe if I delayed it, he would forget. No, I knew he wouldn't forget. But, at least it would give me some time to think about it more, and decide what the right thing to do would be.

"Honest," I said. "I promise I'll tell you tomorrow."

"You'd better," he scowled. He puckered his lips, squinted his eyes and staring at me he added in a sarcastic tone, "I *am* your best friend you know. You should be able to trust me with your precious secret."

I felt both relieved and disappointed in myself.

Douglas moved his feet, rolled back onto them and got off my chest. He stood above me, looking down without a smile. It was an expression I had never seen before. I knew he was disappointed in me. He turned his head, looked around, then went over to where my glasses lay on the ground. He picked them up, brushed them off and handed them to me without looking me in the eye.

"There you go, Clark Kent," he said.

"Thanks," I muttered as I tried to get up. On any other occasion Doug would have reached out a hand and helped me to my feet, but not this time.

Then, the sky opened. The rain poured down on us in buckets. We scrambled and ran down the street. At least we weren't very far from home. It took us about five minutes to get down the hill. We just quickly parted ways and ran for our respective homes.

When I got inside, I went straight to my room, changed my clothes and sat in my stuffed chair. Faced with an important decision, my mind swirled and swirled. Best friend - magic secret - loyalty - to whom? to what? There was a part of me that truly wanted to share the secret with my friend, but another part wanted to uphold the way of the magician: secrecy. Douglas was obviously not very happy with me. He had never been that way before. He was always happy, outgoing, generous. But he had withdrawn. Should I break the magician's oath just because I didn't want to hurt my friend's feelings? Was it worth maybe losing his friendship over a magic trick?

Taking the knife out of my pocket, I held it gently in the palm of my hand. I rolled it over and over, looking at both sides - the white side and the black side. White - black. White - black. Me - Doug. Me - Doug. Friendship - magic. Friendship - magic. Did it come down to that? Friendship or magic? Which was worth more to me? Doug had helped me out of some tight spots. He stuck up for me. But, he had also gotten me into trouble sometimes. But, he was always a friend. A friend. My best friend. I didn't want to lose my best friend. Dave had been my father's best friend. Pa had lost Dave. I didn't want to lose Doug.

Then, I remembered the time that Pa gave Dave the .45 Automatic pistol. Pa really treasured his guns, but he had just given this one to his friend. He didn't offer to sell it to him - he just gave it to him.

I asked my mother if she would drive me to the Joke Shop after supper. I wanted to buy a color-changing knife for Doug. I wanted to be like my father and give my best friend something that he really wanted. Besides, that way I wouldn't be just giving the secret away. Pete, at the joke shop, had told me that when you buy a trick, you buy the secret. So, I'd buy the trick and the secret for my friend. My mother was surprisingly understanding and agreed to drive, even though it was still pouring outside.

The following morning, the sun was shining brightly. I was feeling better, and was excited about giving Doug his magic trick. Shoving the box in my pocket, I went outside and crossed the yard. Standing underneath Doug's window I called.

"Hey, Doug-ay! Come on out!"

There was no response, so I called again.

"Hey, Doug-ay!"

The back door opened and Doug's mother came out. She was motioning with her finger on her lips that I should be quiet. Maybe Doug was asleep. Then, she motioned with her hand for me to come closer.

"Hi, Eddy," she said quietly. "Could you come inside for a moment?"

This seemed very strange. I had never been in Doug's house before. I couldn't understand why his mother was inviting me inside. If he were just asleep, she could have told me to wait and come back later.

"Good morning, Mrs. Collier," I said politely. "Is Doug asleep or something?"

She just shook her head and motioned me inside.

"Follow me," she added softly.

We went through the kitchen and into the living room. Everything was rather dark. There weren't any lights turned on. The room was large, with a big sofa at one end. The cushions on the sofa were well-worn, as was the recliner that sat next to it. There was a fireplace with a mantel that was decorated with family pictures and a few trophies. I didn't have any trophies in my house.

"Have a seat," she said. "Mr. Collier will be down in a moment."

What was going on? Was something wrong? Had Douglas done something really bad and had he been grounded? Why is *Mr.* Collier going to tell me about this? Why couldn't his mother tell me whatever it is? I looked around the room nervously. I felt in my pocket for the knife I was planning to give him. Maybe it had something to do with that. Maybe his father had something against knives. I quickly pulled my hand out. Of course, there was no way that he could know I was going to give Doug a knife.

A few minutes later, Mr. Collier walked into the room. He was tall, slim, and had blond hair, in a crewcut. Even though Doug had lived next to me for several years, I hardly ever saw his father. The expression on his face was very serious. I felt as though I were sinking into the sofa. My stomach began to growl...not because I was hungry, though. And my scalp began to tingle.

"Hello, Eddy," Mr. Collier said as he pulled up the hassock and sat on it, facing me.

81

"Hello, Mr. Collier," I answered.

He put his hand up to his mouth and covered it for a moment. It was like he didn't really want to say what he was about to say. His eyes were dark and somewhat swollen, and he glanced around the room, especially up at the mantel. Finally, he made eye contact with me again.

"Last night, during that terrible rainstorm, Douglas and his older brother went for a drive...the rain was very bad...a real downpour...there was an accident."

He was having difficulty forming his words.

"Donald is in the hospital...his legs are broken...but he's going to be all right."

The growling in my stomach got worse. My head began to throb. My throat tightened. There was a buzzing sound in my ears. I began to sense what was coming, so I began to bite my lower lip. Mr. Collier didn't want to say it and I didn't want to hear it. I could feel my head starting to shake back and forth as a tiny voice somewhere inside me began to say "No! No! No!"

"But, Douglas...Douglas didn't...."

His eyes overflowed with tears as he raised both hands to his head and pushed back his hair.

Now my head was aching and shaking even more. I knew it now. He didn't have to say the words. I knew the words already. I knew he was going to say that Douglas *didn't make it*. The tiny voice wasn't tiny any more. I could hear it with my ears.

"No! No! No! It can't be! Not again"

I didn't want to lose someone else. The tears just gushed out of my eyes. I sobbed and sobbed. He was crying, too, but he was trying to hold it back. Trying to be strong. I didn't need to be strong. I was still a kid. I could let it all out. I slumped over and kept sobbing. Soon, I felt big, warm hands on my back, rubbing my shoulders and my head.

Suddenly, it felt as though I was just falling out of my body, onto the ground, but the ground wasn't there. There was just a big pit, and I was falling headlong into it. Going down, down. But, where? No where. There was no where to go. As I fell, I seemed to see my Father's friend Dave trying to catch me, but he missed. Then Pa tried to catch me, but he missed, too. Finally, Doug was there and he caught my hand. But, his grip was wet and slimy. It kept slipping, and I tried harder to get a better grip. Finally, our fingers just separated and I fell deeper into the darkness.

The next I remember, my mother was standing over me and I

was lying down on something very soft. I must have passed out. My mother was talking to Mr. and Mrs. Collier. She just kept saying how sorry she was and thanking them for something...for calling her. She said she'd take me home. Then, I felt her arms around my shoulders. I could smell her pancake makeup. I knew that smell very well. It smelled good, and safe and comforting.

"Come on, Eddy," she spoke softly to me. "Let's go home."

The entire world changed for me that day. My father was gone. My best friend was gone. I was on my own. For most of the day I just sat in my room. Once I got a slight burst of energy and decided to go outside and do some digging in my cave. At that point it was about five feet deep. I even made a ladder out of some old boards, so I could climb down into the hole. I had recently begun to dig across, horizontally. I planned for a ceiling about two feet thick, so I had about three feet to work with at that point, and I had dug about three feet in, so my cave was beginning to take shape. With shovel and pitchfork on my shoulders, I walked through the tall grass to the cave. When I arrived, my heart sunk.

Because of the previous night's rain storm the "roof" of the cave had...caved in! In addition, the hole was muddy and filled with water. My cave was now just a gross sink hole. I spent a few minutes cursing and shoveling in some of the dirt that had piled up next to the hole. *What a stupid idea this was,* I thought.

Chapter Twelve

The following morning, the sun was shining brightly. I woke up around ten o'clock and stumbled downstairs, still rather groggy. Pouring myself a big bowl of *Frosted Flakes*, I sat down on the couch in the den and watched TV. Nothing interested me that day, so I got dressed and went for a walk, up to the pig nut tree. The walk wasn't the same without Doug. Oh, sure, I had gone there a few times by myself, but we usually went together.

It was getting close to noon, so the sun was directly overhead. At first, I sat with my back up against the tree. The ground was dry by then. I had decided to wear the white sailor's cap that my Uncle Charlie had given me, but I wished that I had worn my cowboy hat...the sun was very strong and hot.

Picking up a nut and rolling it around in the palm of my hand, I wondered why they were called pig nuts. What did pigs have to do with nuts? These nuts didn't look like pigs. Did pigs like to eat these nuts? I took one and cracked it between two stones. The thick shell broke cleanly in half. I examined it closely, then realized that when I looked at it, the open part did look something like a pig's nose. Maybe that was it. Then I tossed it aside. Who cared about pig nuts? I didn't.

I scanned the view. The slope of the hill was just such that I couldn't see any of the houses on the street below. In the other direction, I could always see the shipyard. I hoped that I'd never have to work there myself. People used to say that *everyone* works at the shipyard at one time or another. But not me, I thought. I wasn't going to get poisoned down there, that's for sure.

As I shifted my position, I suddenly felt a sharp pain in my seat. The box with Doug's color changing knife was still in my pocket. I took it out and opened it up. He would have really liked this. It was a great trick. And you get two knives! I took the gimmicked knife out and placed it in the palm of my right hand. Over and over, I made the secret move that changed it from black to white and back again. My life was changing, just like this knife. Yesterday I was just a kid, playing cowboys and Indians, cops and robbers, army, and my favorite superheroes. Today I'm different. I'm not just a kid anymore. Maybe I'm still young, but my world isn't just one of TV and comic books any more. Three people in my life died this summer. Heck, Abraham Lincoln was dead. Some day I'd be dead, too. But, I couldn't think about being dead. Thinking about being dead makes you sad. I don't want to be sad. I want to be happy. I want to be alive.

Sure, the pig nut tree makes me feel safe and secure, but I can't spend my life living under the pig nut tree. I have to come down from the hill. I have to be a part of what I see out there.

I changed the knife from white to black again, then I stood up. Looking at the tree, I saw my first initial etched in the bark, the one I had carved on the day I showed Doug the knife trick. There had only been time to do the first letter. I opened the knife and finished carving my initials in the bark of the tree. Below that, I carved Doug's initials. At the base of the tree, directly below our initials, I carefully placed the knife, thinking that maybe some day, in some way, Douglas would come back to the pig nut tree and the knife would be waiting for him.

Looking out over the horizon, I whispered, "Okay, Doug. Johnny Jet *is* faster than The Flash."

I didn't go back to the pig nut tree again for a very long time.

Author's Notes

The summer of 1960 was, indeed, a year of transition for me. I went from being a child to the beginnings of adulthood. Fortunately, it was not as turbulent in reality as it is in this story.

For me, **Under the Pig Nut Tree** was a labor of love. I'm not even sure I remember just why I started to write it, but once I did, it began to flow. I spent hours and hours searching my memory for the events that are portrayed here.

Because this is a fictionalized memoir, not all of these events actually took place during that summer and not all of the events actually took place. Although the characters are all real, a few names have been changed. While Douglas was a real friend of mine, in this book he is a compilation of several friends from my boyhood.

One of my motivators for writing this book was my own struggle to come to grips with my father's death. He and I were never really close. When he died, I came to realize how little I knew about him. For example, I read in his obituary that he had been in the Battle of the Bulge. Pa never talked about the war. Occasionally I would ask a question, but he was usually evasive. In reality, he died when I was in my fifties.

My hope is that as you, the reader, accompany me on this journey, you will reflect on how precious life is and how precious relationships are, whether they be with siblings, friends or family.

ALSO BY EDWARD L. SCHULTZ